She **Lies** Still

She **Lies** Still
Cassidy Choi

Charleston, SC
www.PalmettoPublishing.com

She **Lies** Still

Copyright © 2022 by Cassidy Choi

All rights reserved.

No portion of this book may be reproduced, stored in a retrieval system, or transmitted in any form by any means–electronic, mechanical, photocopy, recording, or other–except for brief quotations in printed reviews, without prior permission of the author.

First Edition

Hardcover ISBN: 979-8-8229-0348-7
Paperback ISBN: 979-8-8229-0349-4
eBook ISBN: 979-8-8229-0350-0

To Alex, for listening to every word
To Michael, for listening while he could

Table of Contents

The Room Next Door · 1
Daddy's Arm Chair ·9
Night Cap · 17
Driving It Home · 25
Head to Toe ·30
Upstairs · 37
Walking the Dog ·45
Busy Summer ·52
Two of Swords ·60
The Lake House ·65
Bear and Bull · 73
Picture Day ·83
Two Sets of Keys ·90
16 Hours Ahead · 96
Birthdays Abound · 103
A College Party · 112
Welcome Home · 125
Leaving Again · 132
Intermission · 137

Michigan	144
TV Family	153
Let Sleeping Bears Lie	162
Falling Downstairs	171
Austrian Conference	177
Going Rogue	184
Miles To Go	196
Meet the Friend	205
The Weather Man's Home	212
Meet the Parents	220
Bad News	227
Can't Stay	237
Jump	245

The Room Next Door

I delicately grazed my thumb over the rim of my perspiring glass, feeling the drops wrap around my finger from every which way. I welcomed the sensations stimulated from each angle. The coldness on my bare skin, the slight tingle as the drops ran from the inner part of my nail to the bed. Enchanted by the scene before me, net safely in my hands, I could have stayed there the rest of the evening, swooping the glass from palm to palm, letting the drink massage my fingers.

More than my desire for that, though, happened to be what was inside the glass.

I knew I'd need it for what was to come next.

I took a sip.

Swallowing warmth, I eased back into my chair, allowing my forearms to slide forward along the countertop.

The bar itself was playing no music, which only amplified the pounding from the place next door. I felt myself getting nervous, and part of me wanted to stay exactly where I was for the rest of the night.

But, the pounding.

That's not to say that I didn't relish this discomfort. I almost actively seek the types of situations in which I'm forced to take a plunge of some kind. I especially loved feeling like I was part of some deep, seedy underground, no matter how clean and straight the places were. I saw myself as part of a subculture, where people look straight ahead, but never side to side.

This interest was sparked not from an excessive exposure to these types of places, but from my self-taught ability to ignore the grotesque in seemingly innocent places from an early age. Is there a large piece of shit in the ball pit? Well, the only things I'm throwing are brightly colored, so I'll be careful. Did someone throw up in the crawl tunnel in the jungle gym again? No problem, I'm already on all fours, so I might as well lunge over the pile and keep on moving.

This attitude made me realize that if I could turn a blind eye to something unwanted, I could often still enjoy the beautiful things in life, without something from the outside to sully it. Conditions never had to be perfect, and this allowed me to indulge in things just a little bit longer than everyone else, in places that no one else necessarily saw as desirable.

This insufferable longing to find spaces that I wouldn't fit in became a yearning over the years, and by the time I turned 21, I found myself heavily intrigued by strip clubs.

I was fascinated by them. I loved suggesting it to friends at the most inappropriate times, almost jokingly, but also perfectly happy to be called on my bluff.

As a woman, there is a certain amount of trust awarded to you in female strip clubs. During a lap dance or while the dancers are making their rounds, they tend to suggest that I put my hands on them, caress them in ways that a man would assuredly need to pay double for. More often than not, the female dancers allow women to do more, see more, and touch more than the male patrons.

I felt as though I were in a playground where I was able to have more of an experience just because of who I was, where I could have more fun, lunging over others, crawling deeper into the tunnel.

Social norms aside, what I found fascinating were the inconsistencies in rules. No alcohol at Alley Cats. No touching the dancers in Dream Girls. Full nudity in Déjà vu. What you could and could not do varied by city or county, and there almost seemed to be no valid reason for the distinctions.

A Venn Diagram of debauchery that leaves you feeling too perverted to ask the finer details.

I reveled in this, rolled around in the need to know, and often found myself in strip clubs at peculiar times. In this instance, during Easter weekend, two days in a row.

In this particular venue, alcohol couldn't be served in the actual strip club, but there was an accompanying bar next door. The plan was just one drink before checking to see what was on the other side.

Still, the pounding.

The music pumping from the wall behind me made the bar throb, a constant pulsating reminder of the room next door.

Be it a party, a club, or what have you, I've always loved the idea of separating myself from the crowd, only choosing to join when I feel ready. Closing a bathroom door at a club, wondering if I actually want to go out and join my friends on the dance floor, or at a party, finding solace in an empty room, debating whether or not I can sneak out without anyone noticing my absence.

The dull beckoning always reminded me that there's something more on the other side. Something bigger, and more alluring than me.

How arrogant to think that people would notice, or care about my absence?

Part of me knew it was more than that, though. I'd never truly cared if people wanted me around. What was always more important to me was that I wanted others to know that I didn't care about their presence. I wanted people to know that I was perfectly happy without them.

"You know, Catherine, after this, things are going to change between us."

Startled, my eyes shot open. I had forgotten that I wasn't alone.

I tend to do things alone most of the time, sometimes due to my laziness and not wanting to round people up, or because I don't actually have a lot of friends to call on.

Usually, though, because I was doing something that I didn't want others to see. This, normally, would have been of the latter scenarios, yet, here I was. In a here we were.

Of course, he didn't need to acknowledge something so glaring, but I'd assumed we'd felt quite similarly in the car ride north. To be fair, things had already changed. We had made small talk, and dabbled in our usual banter, but the laughter would trail off in an unnatural way that neither of us was quite used to. We always had a light relationship. The back and forth, our shared interests in obscurities, and our ability to share a knowing look from across a room was something unspoken but treasured between us. All this wasn't lost, but misplaced in this moment, as we were suspended in uncertainty and unchartered territory.

Things were different, for sure, but what he meant deep down was the playfulness, the purity of what we have, was soon to be tainted.

Or perhaps, it was never pure. Maybe we were finally peeking behind the curtain to see what was there for us all along.

It was his idea to venture to a strip club out of town, so as not to be recognized. It was the Monday after Easter, so we'd both had the evening free, after only making these plans on a whim the night before. Our conversation last night had gone so smoothly, so coquettishly, as we were now it seemed like we couldn't possibly have been those same people.

Arriving home the previous night from the strip club, I had noticed some messages from Frank at around 2 am. He'd mentioned a book that he thought I'd be interested in, that he'd just been at a small gathering with some of his colleagues and he was feeling a little tipsy. My response to him, so late in the evening, piqued his curiosity as to why I had still been awake. I boasted that I had just gotten home from a strip club and his aptly quick and jarring reply was "Let's go." I had been quite taken by his candor, and sheer adrenaline and excitement coursed through my body. Caught up in the moment, and riding the high, I replied "Tomorrow?"

And here we were. Tomorrow.

I shot him a faux-confident glance as though to communicate that I'd known this, been ready for it, even planned it. I wanted him to see me as cunning, unwavering, and as though I was completely comfortable with the situation.

He'd only ever seen so sure of myself, never giving a fuck and making sure everyone knew it. That's how I wanted him to see me. That's how I wanted everyone to see me.

Frank started again. "Let's do this. We watch some dances, and then after seeing a few of the women, we should each select someone we want a lap dance from, and we'll buy each other a dance."

The forwardness of his suggestion caught me off guard, and I let my eyes widen slightly before turning back toward the bar. Up until that point, he and I had always tiptoed a line, but never crossed it. The line, chucked, allowed us to discuss watching naked women dancing, and how we'd proceed to select one of our favorites and then, essentially, gift each other a dance.

As suspicious as it was that he'd seemed to come up with this idea on the spot, I tried to keep my cool, as if I'd be jaded to any suggestions. I wanted him to think I'd lived, done, and seen it all.

I shrugged just my right shoulder and nodded, still looking toward the shelves of alcohol in front of me. I felt like that made me look self-assured.

He looked at me in awe, and I wanted nothing more than to retain that ideation. My eyes flickered to his, and then to his drink.

"Are you nursing that drink for a reason?"

I moved my narrow straw to the side of my glass, between my ring and middle fingers, and lifted my drink up to my lips before gulping down the remaining liquid.

"There," I thought to myself. "Let's get this over with."

The back of my bare, sweaty thigh dragged against the cheap bar stool, and I immediately felt self-conscious sliding off, and slowly wriggled in a way that would spread and slather my sweat across the seat, hopefully less noticeable to my counterpart, as I eventually found my way off the edge. I hopped off with a bit of confident enthusiasm, hoping the cloth of my yoke skirt would mop up the rest of the moisture. I looked impatiently at the door, and waited for him to take his lingering eyes off of me. His eyes remained on me while he downed his drink.

He slid off his chair with a surprising amount of clumsiness, considering his height, and the fact he was wearing jeans. I couldn't help but notice how much more graceful I'd had appeared—albeit with far more effort and thought—despite the obvious struggle I'd had physically. Scraping 5'2", it was always an endeavor to dismount a bar stool, whereas I assumed he'd had at least a foot on me, and yet his movements still looked childlike. Despite his gangly and wobbly nature, he still seemed surer of proceeding than I did.

Walking out of the bar was an even stranger feeling than being in the bar. I could still hear the disarray from the strip club, but there was also the fresh air, the lack of pounding on the walls, and the view of the car that told me that the choice was still mine. The threshold hadn't been completely crossed or broken.

Yet, I'd come all that way.

I remember being hung over, on my sister's couch, less than a week after I'd turned 21. We had been having a chat about the mere significance of the age. She hadn't actually given me a proper present yet—not that I'd pressed her for one— and she suggested finally getting a tattoo.

"Well, what if we went and got you a tattoo right now?"

And that's one of those things, once you call ahead, express interest, and once you get there, you can't really back out once the needle is ready.

"Granted, I suppose you could apply that same argument to trying heroin for the first time."

"Catherine, what did you say? Are you okay?" Frank asked, a little confused.

Snapping back to reality, I felt my head spin as my blank eyes focused on Frank.

Had I said that out loud? I decided to ignore him.

I glanced at the car, then toward the door, and finally back at Frank. I nodded slowly.

"Are you ready?"

The withdrawal created a longing in my head, and we both veered left and walked into the room next door.

Daddy's Arm Chair

Before I could change my mind, I charged forward, swinging the door to the strip club wide open. Immediately, I was greeted by a blast of music that threw me back into Frank, who was right behind me. The club itself soundless would have been enough to knock me backwards, and I'd felt suddenly unprepared for the environment before me. The club was absolutely massive, with multiple stages, velvety red couches and armchairs, and an empty DJ area that added to the club's peculiar vastness.

Frank explained to me that sitting right in front of the stage implies you'll be tipping a lot, so he suggested we hang toward the back. The intent, of course, was that our main focus would be the lap dances.

We snagged a bench seat and tried to settle in. The music felt somehow more cohesive while actually sitting in the room. Watching the dancers, I couldn't help but feel uncomfortable with Frank next to me. Was he turned on? Was he turned on by me? Should he be? Should I be?

The first time I watched porn I was in middle school. A group of us had gone to a friend's house, who'd bragged about finding a video online and wanted us to watch it together on his laptop. We had all joked, made fun of each other, surmised who'd get a boner first while all slowly easing ourselves into a joint sense of understanding and comfort. A group of six or so of us huddled around a laptop, ready for what was quite likely very new for all of us, we pressed play and watched with bated breath.

Of course, the opening sequence to most pornography is likely to have zero nudity, impossibly bad acting, and a ham-fisted plot, which enabled an immediate relief to fall over the room. Even more so, we could keep joking around with each other, pointing out flaws and heckling the screen.

This, quickly, led us to feel a false sense of comfort, right before the kissing, the rubbing, and the moaning. Our laughing subsided and the hush that fell over the room was drowned out by the subsequent purring of pleasure filling the living room, massaging our ears.

As narrow-minded as it is to assume, I think we all felt the exact same wave of emotions, starting with shock. Things had happened so rapidly that our coping mechanism of chiding each other and the film prevented us from feeling a natural flow of what we should have, and thus, we were hit with the blunt force trauma of a sex scene. After the shock, we started to feel normal. And by normal, I mean horny. Really horny.

Or at least, I did.

I longed to hear the actress moan, craved the way the man thrusted into her as he gripped her hips in this gentle, purposeful way. I got lost in my raging hormones, the tangle of their limbs, and then I remembered: I'm in a room full of other people, watching. After who knows how long, we all snapped back to reality and looked sideways at each other, giggling, watched for a moment longer, and then all decided to pause the video and watch an actual movie instead.

Not that we were dissuaded, though. We just knew it was something we'd want to enjoy in private.

Strip clubs, in a way, are just that junior high school scenario. You watch people with these sort of glazed looks on their faces, intensely turned on— it's almost weirder if they don't look turned on—while you sit quietly and try not to judge.

After each dance, the dancer walks around and chats with the guests, enticing them with her fake name and the suggestion of a lap dance either now, or the next time she comes around. I watched the women, so comfortable and unabashed in their sexuality, and I couldn't help but admire them. Watching them slowly remove skimpy articles of lingerie, deliberate and seductive, I wanted so badly to be just like them.

Not on a stage, but I wanted control over my every movement, and I wanted to know that each move, from a flirtatious laugh, to a sexy glance was giving the illusion of confidence that I'd wanted so much to exude. Unencumbered by the thirsty eyes of the audience, I watched women loll their heads, clutching the pole, sauntering in a circle, tossing their hair in the opposite direction of their waltz, shooting fuck-me eyes to different people at premeditated moments.

It felt funny that something so unfamiliar to me was something I'd desired so badly.

"So, have you decided which one you want?"

The very question snapped me out of my trance. I cringed reflecting on Frank's choice of words. I felt like we were at one of those fresh seafood restaurants, and I'd been tasked with selecting a lobster from the inhumanely small tank. I remember the waiter would always suggest choosing ones from the top, the ones who writhed and wiggled and still had some fight in them.

"Those are healthier so they taste the best."

One of the dancers had come over to us multiple times, and I'd decided her efforts deserved some pay off, and made eye contact with Frank. I coyly tucked my hair behind my ear and glanced over at her, motioning toward her with my chin.

Frank shot me an understanding look, and used his actual fingers to flag her down. She walked over, and we discussed the terms of the dance, how long it'd be, and how much it would cost. As this would actually be my first lap dance, the exchange felt dry and transactional. It struck me as odd at the time, but I was sucked back into the moment once the business was squared away, and then, looking at Frank, she asked if he wanted to watch us.

It hit me half a second too late that she was offering Frank the opportunity to watch her give me a lap dance, and when he'd said yes, my jaw dropped.

I had assumed that we'd buy each other a lap dance, let the person enjoy themselves in peace, and we'd meet back up with the mutual understanding that we would only discuss the happenings on a superficial level, and maybe laugh about something vulnerable here and there on the way home.

She grabbed my hand and started leading us to a sectioned off area toward the back of the main room, away from the stage. In a dark corner, I felt myself trembling. I wasn't sure whether or not to look back at Frank and shoot him a sexy glance, or something more pleading—something suggesting that I was in over my head and he won our game of chicken—or if I should merely stare straight ahead, confident in my convictions.

Still shaking, I let her seat me in a large, red leather armchair, positioned in such a way where there was another one just like it, facing me. Frank took that seat. The chair, as it were, was comically large for me. My feet hovered a good five inches off the ground if I leaned back all the way, and leaning forward would have amounted to not allowing enough space for the dancer to position herself on top of me.

I felt stupid, hating my skirt, knowing that, my arms barely reaching the end of the arm rests, with my legs spread wide, I'd looked like a little girl who snuck into her father's office to sit in his chair. I was trying to be a big girl.

My legs were even splayed out in that careless way little girls sit before society tells them to sit up tall, cross your legs, and don't go out with your professors to strip clubs.

I decided to lean back, and try not to think. She was nice enough to let one song finish before starting my lap dance, which was ample time for me to overthink how idiotic and out of place I felt. I'd tried to see if hugging one side of the chair was a better, more comfortable position, but no matter what, I'd looked hopeless, each rearrangement like a rat trying to climb out of a cage.

Nowhere to run, I glanced over at Frank, who'd fit into his chair of the same size perfectly. His long legs were even able to create an acute angle as his knees bent upward toward his chest, to connect his inner thighs perpendicularly to his elbows, projecting his arms upward so that his hands cradled the bottom half of his face. I watched him for a moment, while his hands took turns covering all or parts of his face. Frank looked rattled. I couldn't tell which one of us was more anxious. I felt the tension in my shoulders release.

If he was suffering, he wouldn't see me suffering. This, in turn, made me feel more relaxed.

It was always more important to me that people didn't see how miserable I was, more so than whether or not I was actually feeling miserable.

The rough song transition signified a new song, and the dancer began our transaction. At that moment, Frank, head still in his hands, lifted his eyes and met mine for a second. I looked away, thinking I'd look much cooler if I was only staring at her, watching how she moved, staring at her face when it felt natural to do so. I knew that I needed to look like I didn't need his approval.

I gazed up at her, while she writhed and started stroking my neck. She nibbled on my ear. I felt her drizzling all over my body. She whispered that I could touch her anywhere, and I lost control for a moment, my eyes closing, but not before they rolled backward.

My head jerked lightly and I shivered, and for the next two minutes and thirty seconds, I thought only about her body on me, while desire swirled through my head. Feeling her lips on my skin, I tightened my eyes and imagined exactly what her mouth looked like, each divot in her lips, moist and plush, catching the baby hairs on my neck. I trembled like the little girl I had felt like mere moments before. Her fingers were firm, and she pressed into me with intention and desire, as she began to sink down further on top of me. I gasped and flashed my eyes up at her.

She put both hands around the back of my neck, forcing my face up to hers. She buried my face into her neck. I let my breathing intensify, and could feel the hairs on the back of her neck stand up, her skin stimulated with goosebumps. I'd moved my hands up around her waist, fingering her bra strap. She grabbed my hands and placed them directly onto her breasts. I fidgeted with the lace at the top part of her bra cup as she guided my fingers inside her bra to rub her nipples.

I felt the entirety of her. Desire to taste her overwhelmed me, wanting to lift the cup to my lips. Moving my face toward her chest, I rested my mouth against her and began to lightly kiss the feast before me.

The song ended abruptly, and the façade was quickly dropped while she dismounted me and turned around to ask Frank for her money. He had handed her the payment, plus a tip. Looking satisfied, she led us back to the common area, where we retrieved our previous seats.

"You looked like you really enjoyed that," Frank said, breaking the silence a little too long after the dance.

My chest still heaving, I gave Frank a weak smile, my cheeks hot.

I'd felt very seen, very vulnerable.

"It was nice to see you like that," he added.

I'd imagined myself in that living room in middle school, surrounded by my friends watching porn. If I had turned to my left and saw my friend staring at me, watching me in awe with the video, I would have been furious at him, or looked away sheepishly.

At least, I think I would have. But what if I hadn't? What if I liked being seen like that? If only, of course, I knew I was being watched. Then, I'd be able to control what he saw. How he saw me.

In an effort to compose myself, I shot back, "Okay, now it's your turn."

It didn't take him long to hone in on his target.

"Her," he'd said, definitively.

She had walked by uninterested a few times prior, however, seeing us stumble back from the armchairs seemed to spark more interest in us. She gave us slightly more pointed attention, not realizing we had been waiting for her, and that she really only had to be near enough for us to beg for her attention again.

Me, because I wanted to see Frank squirm and feel as exposed as I did. For him—at least, from my perspective—because he wanted her. Badly. She made her way over, and when she asked if we wanted anything from her, the look I gave Frank was almost pleading.

"Please," my eyes said, "tell her what you want."

Like clockwork, as though we'd forgotten something we so desperately needed to retrieve, we walked back into the den.

Night Cap

The woman he chose was noticeably—to me—more than a decade my senior. She was petite, pale, with dark features. Her straight brown hair was pulled taut to a ponytail, which seemed more tactical than sexy, as though her job were coaching a soccer team, as opposed to enchanting men for money.

Frank sat comfortably in the very chair I'd been squirming in moments ago, and his three minutes in heaven started soon after. As I now didn't have to worry about another person on top of me, I tried to copy what Frank had done while I was receiving my dance. He had been leaning forward, head in his hands. I started to mimic him, inching my feet downward so that they could finally touch the ground. I felt as though I looked like I was really getting comfortable for the show, but something still didn't feel quite right.

I decided, instead, to lean into the juxtaposition of my stature in the chair, and I swung one leg over the other, my left arm extended upward from the armrest, my head rested against my fist. The right side of the armchair may not need to exist, as far as I was concerned. If I couldn't take up enough space, I'd make it look like I didn't need it or want it anyway. It dawned on me that I didn't quite know what I was supposed to do. Was I supposed to watch him, as he'd watched me? Or was I supposed to watch her?

One look at his face, and I immediately knew I'd rather look anywhere else.

In all of our time together, I'd never seen that look on his face. On any man's face, really. He knew exactly where to look at her, how to look at her, and I felt far too intrusive. A voyeur. I was invading his privacy, and at a moment's notice, he could catch me gawking at him. The shame was almost too much for me to bear.

I decided the safer route was to continue to watch the dancer, because that'd make me look cool, like I was admiring her movements and fixated and attracted to her. I was afraid of what staring at Frank would communicate to him.

Would he think I was turned on by watching him? Did he think I was turned on right now?

I had been so captivated by my dance, I didn't even notice who or what Frank had been looking at.

By agreeing to this adventure, what was that conveying to him, truly? I could feel my pulse quickening, thinking of all of the ways in which I hadn't thought ahead. I'd been so excited by the idea of agreeing to his suggestion because it was so out of the blue, so peculiar that a professor would ask me to go to a strip club with him a month before graduation that I didn't even think about the repercussions.

What was this communicating to him? What did it mean to me? I felt a lump in my throat and resigned myself to taking the rest of the evening as it came. I was in it, and I wasn't going to back down now. As much as I wanted to leave, I found myself wanting to see this through to the end. I took a deep breath to calm my nerves, and reset.

I focused my gaze on the dancer, and wondered what drew Frank to her. I knew he had been married before, but I knew nothing of the types of women he liked.

I wondered if he was trying to communicate something to me by selecting her. She was thinner than I, but we had the same basic build. We're both pale, although my face is littered with freckles. We both have light brown hair. I wondered if he wanted me to see that he wanted someone who looked quite similar to me. Or, did he notice our differences? Was he trying to tell me that he wanted someone more like her? Thinner, more confident?

Amidst an orchestra of doubt in my head, I noticed the song in the room had changed, and Frank and I happened to be sucked back into reality at the same time. I gave him a gentle smile, and approached his throne. I handed the dancer her payment and she looked knowingly at Frank, to me, and smiled. As Frank started to stand, I heard a surprisingly high-pitched, chipper voice come from the dancer.

"Do you want a dance together?"

She sounded like someone who'd yell at a cashier for no reason. I knew my choice to fixate on her voice was only because I didn't want to face the actual question she'd asked. Do we want a dance together? I was also aware of the money in my wallet, or lack thereof, but didn't want to admit that I didn't have enough cash on me. I glanced at Frank who seemed far less inhibited than I was.

He was eager, even, and he looked at the dancer and asked in a very in-the-know kind of a way, "what are we looking at here?" She explained that she'd want forty dollars for three minutes, which gave me an excuse to peek into my wallet. I had one twenty left. For a moment, I thought we'd been free, but it occurred to me that we were still in it, and I'd committed to seeing this through until the end. I looked at Frank, whose eyes begged me. I gave him a gentle smile and nodded.

"So, what does this entail, exactly?"

My question sounded uncomfortably formal, and I'd regretted saying it as soon as both Frank and the dancer shot me the same accusing look. Was there some kind of strip club jargon that I hadn't been coached on?

"Well," the dancer mused, almost as though she hadn't thought about the mechanics until now, "you can sit on his lap, and I'll dance on both of you."

Frank, still seated, moved further back on the chair, slithering his arms over the back, as though he were soaking in a hot tub. I turned around and slowly sank back into him, overly aware of how close my face was to his. I turned my head slightly to give him a smirk, completely unable to contain how terrified I was feeling. I had even started shaking again, which I imagine he couldn't help but notice as well.

Every wall I'd had up, any picture of myself I'd tried to paint was completely demolished. I felt so childish, so transparent. Had I really thought I could handle this?

Frank brought one hand to my shoulder and gave it a little squeeze, and I turned back around, our faces nearly touching. I looked forward and reminded myself it'd only last three minutes.

Everything in life ends. One way or another.

The music started and the dancer, facing me, wrapped her arms around my neck, draping them over as she started grinding on me, taking her time to find space on either side of Frank's thighs to slide her own into the crevasses of the cushion. Her hands still wrapped around me, she tousled my hair, taking breaks to caress Frank's face. I felt a small bit of tension around the outer side of my right breast.

That can't be right. How could she be massaging my back and groping my breast at the same time?

My eyes snapped downward to see the same hand that'd given me such a reassuring squeeze moments earlier was now fondling my chest. My attention rapidly changed from focusing on what I was even supposed to be doing, sandwiched between two people who both felt like they wanted something from me, to what I was feeling underneath me. As the couch shifted, I could feel his left hand moving toward my hips, and I moaned in a sort of unintentional way. The way you moan when you don't really think about it, uncontrollable but not startling, as his lap started to feel much harder. He was digging into me, but unable to move enough comfortably, I could only shift slightly without pulling the rug out from under our dancer, and I found his erection nuzzled warmly up my skirt, perfectly centered.

Completely overstimulated, I felt oddly comforted by feeling him pushing into me, finding something to focus on. All I thought about was the sensation of his desire for me, knowing that I could mentally make it out of this if I focused on the parts I wanted.

I moved my hips subtly, and looked back at him, first meeting his gaze, then inhaling as I glimpsed at his lips, which were open and longing, then I turned around. I heard him whimper at my tease and felt all that much more powerful.

The song ended, and I slowly hopped off of Frank, and turned around to meet his gaze. He looked a bit shaken, taking far too long to stand up. The dancer and I gave him his privacy and both turned toward each other. She and I shared a laugh, looking downward and around the room at nothing in particular to avoid looking at each other.

"Have you been together long?"

"No, well, we actually..."

I trailed off long enough for Frank to stumble over and hastily remove his wallet from his back pocket. I used that as an excuse not to answer and looked down into my purse to fish out my own wallet. I handed Frank the twenty, in the hopes that he'd do the honors of handing over the money, and thus the responsibility of giving her the tip.

I started to walk away, and as Frank handed her the money, she caught him by the wrist, demanding a larger tip. He hurriedly handed over a few more ones, which didn't seem to satisfy her, so he coughed up a few more. She whispered something to him, and he walked up to me, still shaken and said "Well, she's a really good sales person."

Frank and I both scuttled outside, avoiding the faces of anyone else left in the building. I flung the door open, and the night sky greeted me with open arms, which I swatted away as I stomped to the passenger side of Frank's car without looking back at him. He walked up at his own pace, and unlocked the door for us. Buckling in our seatbelts, I avoided his face.

To be fair, he may have also been doing the same, but I wouldn't have known.

I couldn't bear to look at him just yet.

He put his right arm on the back of my headrest, turning around to reverse, and I stole a glance at his hand.

These were the same fingers that have graded my essays, that have given me feedback, and now, they've massaged my breasts.

The ride back to his house was quiet. Frank would make an occasional witty observation, and I allowed an empty chuckle to keep the peace. The car ride would have felt longer, but my fear of wondering how we would officially end the night made it so that time sped up so I'd have to endure that decision.

I've found that time flies faster when there's a pressing matter at hand that I'm deeply dreading.

We pulled up to the curb directly outside of his house. Without a word, I started walking toward my car. Mid-stride, I heard Frank croak from behind me.

"She told me she thinks we're good together."

I turned back to look at Frank, who took a step toward me.

"After she asked for a bigger tip, she thanked me and said that she thinks we're really good together."

What he said felt loaded, and I knew whatever my reaction would be would transmit a specific message to him. The issue was I didn't know what message I wanted him to receive. Did I want him to know that I thought tonight was a mistake? Or that I was in way over my head? Was that even the case?

"Well, we aren't together, though. So, what she said doesn't really matter anyway."

Frank's face fell, and because I decided not to play ball, he knew he'd have to be more assertive.

"Do you want to come inside for a night cap?"

There it was. And although I had started to feel a little more at ease, and a little more in my element, I chose to decline.

"I think I should go home. I'm pretty beat."

Frank seemed understanding, nodded, and he waved me off. Unlocking my car, I sat down in the driver's seat, and cranked the engine. With no hesitation, I pressed severely on the gas and sped off, not even a glance behind me.

Driving It Home

The road from his house to the onramp is a straight shot, which makes it all too easy to completely floor it down the road. Instead, I took a detour that involved the most immediate left, veering me slightly off course toward my apartment. My unnecessary need to be out of sight awarded me enough time to sit, steeped in my thoughts.

The first of which was "holy shit."

I ran through the rolodex of events in my mind, the memories were frozen. Photographs instead of a movie, my thought-stills flipping like a kineograph.

I had driven to his house, and he'd already been waiting outside, eagerly, to immediately enter his car to drive together. Normally, when I'd come over, he'd at least go through the trouble of normal pleasantries, yet tonight had started with him chomping at the bit to leave. I had always enjoyed his hospitality, his jubilant warmth, and having that replaced so suddenly with an impatient hunger made me uneasy. Haphazardly, I'd moved from my driver's seat to his passenger seat before setting off north.

I stopped at the newly turned red light.

Then, there had been the awkward drive up to the strip club, in which, whatever wall that had been up between us was slowly starting to crumble, and neither of us quite knew how to cope with it. We had tried small talk, although we were never much for small talk to begin with, so it only made us both look like we had no idea what to do with the detritus that had fallen between us.

I stared out the window, enjoying the trek somewhere unfamiliar. I watched as the freeway lamps melted into traffic lights, and as the architecture erected around me in run-down buildings. Gas stations. Dollar sushi restaurants. Abandoned buildings and motels jogged past my window while I gazed outside, the smoothness of the ride only interrupted by sporadic and deliberate throat-clearings coming from the seat to the left of me.

My left hand flipped my blinker downward, and returned back to the steering wheel. I glanced forward briefly, and seeing no headlights, turned left.

We had then had a discussion with the door man, who had explained that there was no alcohol allowed inside the premises. However, our entrance fee would also include a drink ticket for the bar attached, with a separate entrance. The three of us exchanged looks, with the same resolve to the situation, two of us handing over twenty-five dollars in cash and receiving two coupons each in return.

Peering over my right shoulder, I flipped my left hand up lazily as I smacked the blinker upward, moving carelessly toward the on ramp.

There had been the discussion, in the bar, and how things would change from that point forward. I'd feigned confidence, I think, or had I? How had I felt? I couldn't remember how I had felt. Hadn't I been excited? Perhaps I had been just as eager to get to the club as he'd been while waiting for me outside of his house.

I wasn't sure if I'd been remembering things incorrectly, or if I'd been making excuses now that the situation had passed. Since I'd conquered it, was I remembering it in a slightly more pleasant manner than when I had been experiencing it in real time?

I thought I had wanted to puke while it was happening, but the more time passed, the more I remembered enjoying it. With every flip through tonight's photo album, I looked back on everything fondly.

I slowed down, peered over my left shoulder, and after seeing no oncoming cars, I pulled off the off-ramp and rejoined the streets.

He'd wanted to go somewhere out of town so that neither of us would be recognized. It wasn't necessarily inappropriate for either of us individually to be at a strip club, but us together would certainly raise a few eyebrows. Especially if we'd been spotted by people who knew both of us.

And yet, hadn't that been the case?

One of the dancers, the one with olive skin and long, black hair kept glancing over at us during her stage time. I had ducked my head toward Frank and asked in a whisper if she was also a student at school. She had looked so familiar, and the way she kept shooting looks at us seemed to confirm that. I couldn't quite place her, but I couldn't shake the sinking feeling that we had been found. Frank turned toward me, and confirmed my sentiments: she looked familiar, and the way she kept looking at us seemed to support that instinct. After her dance, when most dancers would be making their rounds, offering lap dances, she approached every other party, tactfully avoiding us.

Or had I imagined that?

I remembered some strange story where an American man, while traveling on business, decided to hire a call girl to come to his hotel room. Upon opening the door, he was shocked to discover that the woman he'd hired unseen was his own daughter. I hope to dismiss several potential endings to the story, however, the most interesting point to me was how they were essentially at a stalemate. I'm sure the daughter was furious to know her father had been willing to cheat on his wife, her mother. As I'm sure the father had been shocked to see his own daughter, had been lying about her career. But neither one could out the other, for fear of outing themselves.

Despite our best efforts to not be recognized, we'd been spotted. However, so had she. She'd probably, just as we had, chosen a venue far enough away from people who'd known her so as not to be discovered. There was no way either party would nark on the other, all told by her unwillingness to approach our entire side of the room after her dance. If someone at school had approached either Frank or me about the excursion, I'd have an easy retort.

The red left arrow vanished from the night sky, and I hit the gas, turning left.

Then there were the dances we were offered, and accepted. How embarrassed I'd been, but how good it felt. How we'd each had two dances, or one and a half, and—his hand. I felt his hand massaging my right breast while I was sandwiched between him and the dancer. Did I like it? I was so shocked by it at first, I hadn't really considered if it'd felt good at all. I didn't ask him to stop, but would I have under any other circumstance? Did that mean that I liked it? Or did that mean I didn't know what I wanted?

And, at feeling him caress me, didn't I slowly turn around so he could see my profile?

And hadn't I made eye contact with him, while inhaling lightly, so that my lips trembled and let out a soft moan?

I couldn't remember.

I turned left into the parking lot of my apartment complex.

I sat, shaking, trying to process everything that happened within the last day. Not even 24 hours ago, I had just been a student, graduating in a few weeks, who happened to exchange some odd messages between her professor here and there. My breasts had remained untouched by him, my face had always remained an appropriate distance from his, and he'd certainly never seen how my eyes looked while rolled back. Now, things were different. I was different.

I had been so quick to run away, to flee the scene without further discussion with Frank about what'd happened. I knew that if I had agreed to the night cap, there wouldn't have been much insight into the night. I knew that I was the only person willing to sit and discuss with myself about what happened.

Thinking of what the night cap would entail, I began to feel a warmth in my stomach. An excitement rose within me. Part of me wanted to restart my engine, call Frank, and drive back over to his house.

I wanted to see him, in the pitch-black night, waiting hungrily for me on the porch. His lightly tanned skin, illuminated by the street lights, beckoning for me from afar.

I knew the next time I walked through his door, I'd crawl deeper into the tunnel, and I'd finally see what's on the other side.

Head to Toe

The subsequent weeks flew by in a whirlwind of final exams, a senior thesis, and pumping out the final newspaper of the school year. I'd been busy saying my goodbyes, taking in the large brick building known as Old Main, and the towering trees of the Pacific Northwest before graduation.

Frank and I had been exchanging plain acknowledgements over the last few days, our discussions quickly resembling our previous relationship, and I resigned myself to my normal pre-graduation excitement. The secret of our journey north would remain just that: a secret between an unlikely duo.

Then, through one of our exchanges, the discussion took an unexpected turn.

"Do you want to come over and watch a movie?"

Although I'd started to make peace with the fact that I'd be living out the traditional university graduation experience, I did find myself wondering why things felt like nothing had happened. Why I'd felt lulled into a false sense of normalcy. Perhaps he was feeling me out? Or, very likely, maybe the switch had been flipped, and no matter what, there was no turning back. The normalcy I'd felt was us both being preoccupied by the end of the year. It was only me who didn't understand that we'd gone past the point of no return, and truly, how else did I expect him to talk to me? Just walk up to me and grab my breast from behind?

I quickly obliged. I asked if Friday night worked for him, and we'd agreed on drinks and a movie. The end of my senior year of university fast approaching, in which I'd finished everything due and then some, completed with five years' worth of credits fulfilled within the normal four years. My schedule wasn't nearly as jam packed as the previous semester and although this would be every senior's dream, it certainly made the week drag on a lot longer before Friday.

My Friday was unbearable with anticipation. I'd only had one class—at 11:00—and stayed on campus in the newspaper office to keep occupied. I'd finalized reports, editing news articles for next year, all while busying myself until around 3:00 before leaving. I'd even considered staying until rush hour traffic to elongate my commute, burning more time before stepping foot inside my apartment.

Carefully opening the front door, I removed my shoes, and stuck them into the coat closet. I made my way to the bedroom to grab my toiletries bag and then headed to the bathroom. Turning on lights from each direction, I propped myself up onto the counter. I looked closely at my face in the mirror, aimlessly rummaging through my toiletries for what felt like tweezers, all while never taking my eyes off of my own reflection.

I scrutinized my mug for a stray eyebrow or mustache hair, violently plucking out anything that looked dark enough to see at a close enough range. I began smoothing out round areas of my face, pulling my skin up and down while they caught different angles in the light to see which hairs would be visible from different directions, not caring that it'd be evening when I arrived at his house, and the lights would probably be dim. If our faces were close enough, as they had been while I was sitting on his lap, I wouldn't want him to notice a rogue hair. I wanted him to focus on the parts of me I wanted him to. The good parts.

I imagined my flaws under a microscope, as I think many people do. Intimacy only amplifies the shame of someone noticing your imperfections, and I'd always found that, despite deep preparation, I'd always forgotten or overlooked something. I figured fresh eyes would catch anything that'd gone unnoticed.

I'd next decided that I wouldn't eat. If he had his hands around my waist, I'd want him to feel me as willowy, maybe even with a bit of my ribs peeking out, so he would find me more attractive. I imagined the dancer whom he'd chosen at the club, who'd been a lot more taut and trim than I found myself to be. I thought about him stroking my breast, and thought hard to remember if he'd felt my waist at all. Did he already know what I felt like?

I thought about the bra I'd been wearing, completely unpadded. I'd have to go in like that moving forward. He'd already known what my breast felt like, and there was no hiding it if and when my top came off.

It was better to be up front about those things.

I'd opted for something lacy, revealing, and decidedly unpadded.

I laid my bra on the bed, and moved toward another drawer, where I selected a black thong with a lace band. I tossed it onto the bed, and moved swiftly to my closet. I'd wanted to wear something unassuming, but I especially wanted everything I chose to be easy to remove. Nothing skin tight that would make me overly self-conscious about any bulging. I cringed imagining him struggling to yank down skinny jeans, knowing how difficult it must have been for me to squeeze into them in the first place.

I'd settled on some dark jeans, a red blouse with black edging, and a black military jacket, with an oddly structured silhouette, and tossed those on the bed with my underthings.

I worked my way back toward the bathroom, and checked my face again, before deciding maybe a shower would soften my skin and make certain hairs surface, or soften some hairs that I would otherwise be unable to see.

Disrobing, carelessly tossing my garments to the floor, I hastened inside the shower, too impatient to wait for the water to get warm. I pumped my shampoo into my cupped palm, and massaged it into my scalp. After a rinse, I grabbed my conditioner and squirted liberal amounts of it into my hand, and worked it meticulously into my sopping wet hair. I then grabbed my loofah cloth and my body wash, covering my body with suds and bubbles. I double took as I remembered my next process, shaving. I looked at my razor, and down at my unkempt pubic hair. I was suddenly at a loss for what route to take.

My general go-to was to shave my pubic hair completely, seeing as most men would prefer that to a full bush. That, and because I've always been deeply insecure about my body hair. The hair on my head has always been light brown, silky, soft, and I'd always gotten compliments on it. My body hair, on the other hand, was thick, coarse, and black, taking up far more surface area than I'd like to admit.

A secret I'd wanted to take to my grave, my pubic hair, when untamed looked like a menacing thicket of thorny vines covering a dark cavernous hollow. It looked threatening, uninviting, and more often than not, I thought it better if it were just gone.

Frank is older, 43 to be exact, and I wasn't sure what he'd prefer. Perhaps he'd want something more natural, more 1970's free and uninhibited. In the end, after propping my legs up on various shelving, I felt satisfied with my exhaustive shave. I rinsed out the conditioner, letting the water run over the remaining unwanted hair that still clung to my skin.

Stepping out of the shower onto the bath mat, I immediately soaked the rug, while reaching behind me for the towel. I thoughtlessly wiped my body down, and wrapped my hair into the towel, staring at my bare body in the mirror. My eyes jolted toward a black hair on my upper lip, and upon realizing it was just a shaved pubic hair that somehow made the journey to my face, I primly flicked it off of my lip.

Making my way back toward my bedroom, I flung the towel onto my desk chair, and headed for the garments on my bed. First, I slid my thong up around my ankles, grazing my ass before adjusting the band flatly against my hips. I grabbed my bra, and bent slightly forward, giggling while thinking of my grandmother, who when I was 18, asked if I knew how to put on a bra.

"Well, jeez, grandma. I've been doing it for years. I sure hope so."

Looking at me skeptically, she explained, step by step.

"First, lean forward, at a 90-degree angle. That way, your breasts are completely out. Also, your back fat will move toward your boobs, so that'll add more volume to your cleavage."

I watched my grandmother mime the whole process for me, fully clothed, acting out each part in case I couldn't grasp her explanation verbally.

I glanced over at my full-length mirror at my reflection, chuckling to myself hunched over at an angle, putting on my bra. I stood upright, admiring my grandma-inspired bust, and felt too sexy to get fully dressed. I had been avoiding checking my phone, but decided an update on the outside world was due. Unlocking my screen, I saw a message from Frank, from 20 minutes prior.

"CCC, headed home from school. I'll be ready in an hour. See you soon?"

I looked over at my forlorn clothes on the bed, and my deflating bosoms, and texted back that I'd start heading over in about thirty minutes.

Hastily, I tugged up my jeans, buttoned up my blouse, and threw on my jacket. I hurried to the bathroom and started to brush out my hair, trying simultaneously to scan over my reflection for any noticeable flaw.

Any readily apparent point of embarrassment.

Truly, the answer was everything was embarrassing. How presumptuous had I been about this whole situation? For all I knew, we were just watching a movie. This hadn't been the first time he'd invited me over, and we watched a movie, while drinking. Alone. Together. This had happened before. I stared at myself in the mirror, my vision blurring, the minutes passing.

I blinked myself back to the bathroom. I looked dejectedly away at my own reflection, and began preparing to leave. I began moving my essentials from my backpack into my purse, and, too ashamed to look at my full reflection again in my bedroom,

Cassidy Choi

I made my way to the front door. I swung open the coat closet, grabbed the same pair of shoes, and pulled them on without tying them. Slamming the front door shut, I locked it quickly, and without once looking up from the pavement, I watched my shoe laces bounce around sloppily while making my way to my car.

Upstairs

Pulling up to Frank's house, I half expected him to be waiting outside for me, and the tender feeling of disappointment set in when I parked in front of an empty patio. Turning off the ignition, I peeked up at his picture window, and saw his head glistening, pacing back and forth, rearranging pillows on his sofa, adjusting coffee table books, double taking when a potential threat or oversight popped into his mind. I rested my head against my steering wheel, watching him rubbing his fingers across his mouth, cupping his chin.

Watching him squirm and fuddle around his living room made me realize he'd been just as nervous as I'd been. Only he didn't watch me contort myself in my shower. Letting out a little sigh, I moseyed on over to his front door. Knowing that he'd undoubtedly see me through the window before knocking, I paused in front of his picture window, waiting to catch his eye. Not a moment before I paused, he looked up at me, and I waved comically by wiggling just my fingers. He smirked and stumbled over to the door to let me in.

"CCC, thanks for coming."

His voice always sounded the same as it did during his lectures. A bit booming, although not aggressive. There was something magnetic and engaging about the way he spoke, as though everything he said were not only true, but important and insightful. And when he spoke to you, he had a way of making you feel like there was no one else in the room, you and only you.

But he made every person in the room feel like that.

Stepping into his living room, removing my shoes, I felt a sudden rush of familiarity. It was comforting to see his living room arranged in the same manner that I'd always seen it. He'd always been the type of professor who'd have students over at his place, hosting dinners, establishing a sense of friendship and intimacy that could only really be enabled through a small university environment.

I'd been over a handful of times, multiple times in group settings, sharing his affections with others.

I'd also been over a few times on my own.

The most recent, actually, had been prior to his sabbatical, where he had spent six months in Latvia, studying and teaching at a university there. I remembered feeling disappointed that one of my favorite professors would be gone for the first half of my final year of university.

Little did I know we'd be making up for lost time during my final weeks.

My eyes swept over the living room, stopping at the sectional, before I finally was able to make eye contact with Frank. He looked at me lovingly, his eyes reflecting a kindness I had never experienced before. It actually required effort for me not to hug him, to bury my face into his chest. We'd hugged before, numerous times, but I'd felt as though, having already crossed a certain line, any physical touch would signal more than what it had before. I refrained, and inquired about the drink I'd been promised. Chuckling, he extended his arm toward his kitchen.

He had made a makeshift bar on top of his stove and countertop, and I couldn't help but wonder if all adults always had alcohol on hand, impressed by the average adult's ability to refrain from chugging a whole bottle of something once they'd purchased it. Why did adults always have so many gently sampled alcohol bottles on hand?

I couldn't imagine an older, more established version of myself having enough of anything to offer guests. I'd felt as though anything I'd owned, everything I'd had was meant for me, and only me.

Yet before me, there was an array of hard alcohols, mixers, bitters, and other flavorings. I felt overwhelmed by my options.

After turning 21, I'd decided that I'd needed a drink to call my own, something that made me seem seasoned at the bar, and I didn't want to order anything too high maintenance; working in food service and having bartender friends told me how much of a pain it is to make someone Old Fashioneds and Bloody Marys all night. I'd settled on gin and tonics as my to-go, mainly because I thought they were the healthiest.

I think I heard someone say that in a movie once.

I'd realized we'd be responsible for making our own drinks, and I wasn't sure how much of what to put into my glass. I poured a generous amount of gin into my cup, figuring that I could nurse this drink, without having to get off of the couch and make another later.

Finishing off my kindergarten attempt at a gin and tonic, I scurried on over to the couch and thudded down, legs flopping upward and crossing animatedly. Frank smiled and shook his head, always completely bewildered by my ability to get comfortable.

It was hard for me to determine when I could feel cozy with him, or with anyone, as my boundaries and thought-processes allowed me to weave in and out of comfort, seemingly at random.

In that moment, though, the nerves escaped me, and I waited for Frank to prepare his own drink. Whisky on the rocks. His choice seemed intentional, as I'd never seen him drink something quite so overtly masculine. Figuring that his drink had been just as thought out as mine made me sink deeper into the couch, curling my legs up, sweeping them to the side of me.

A cat saddled and purring on her throne.

Frank eventually sat down on the other end of the sectional, attempting the same floppy fashion I had, but his gangly limbs made him look a bit unwieldy. I laughed, but perhaps not in the way he'd intended.

We chatted about the end of the year festivities, and I'd wished I'd had more to update him on, but truly, the end of the year was uneventful for me. I'd mentioned the newspaper, and how we were working on our final issue of the school year. He'd complimented the great work we'd done that year, another student of ours advocating aggressively for professors to make more money, comparing the various Deans and higher-level staff members making more than five times what the professors do, with either equal or lesser education. He'd discussed as well, how busy he'd been grading papers, helping students edit their essays and writing recommendation letters for graduate school.

"That's the difference between the arts and the sciences! You lot get to take tests and that's it. We have to write, edit, and write, ad nauseum. For you, once you're done, you're done."

I rolled my eyes reactively, and scoffed. He and I had always jokingly been at each other's throats about who'd had things harder in terms of institutional education. Having been a mathematics major, he'd make fun of me for choosing that life for myself.

Ironically, I hadn't the slightest idea what I'd wanted to do in terms of my degree, so as far as calling me out for the life I'd chosen for myself, I'd argue that it'd make more sense for me to be reprimanded for not having yet chosen a life for myself.

"You always fucking talk as though English majors are better than everyone. Could you all be any fuller of yourselves?" I said, giggling to soften my swearing.

He'd been used to it by now, but the way I weave profanity into my normal, unemotional sentences was always jarring to people at first. He laughed.

"No, not at all! The world needs people like you, of course."

"Yeah, but you say that from a god-damn high horse, like 'we need people like you, like we need people who are willing to be janitors.'"

He let out a roaring bark, doubling over in an explosion of laughter. Not only had he been unable to formulate a retort because of his amusement, but he knew deep down, he couldn't refute my argument. I threw my body backward with glee in winning our back and forth, and took a swig of my drink. Gathering himself, he asked if I was ready to start the movie.

Halfway through, Frank asked if we could pause it so he could top off his drink. As he stood up from the couch, I glanced down at my drink, untouched since the victory of the debate, and after taking a few gulps, I decided to polish it off so I could get another one as well.

I slunk up behind him, watching his bouldering shoulders hunch over his stove, this time mixing together something more his style, a mojito. Despite my initial disapproval of his first drink choice, I'd decided to lightly mock his current one.

"Cute drink!" I teased.

He gave me a shy look, and I could see his cheeks had gone a bit ruddy, his eyes slightly glossy, and I'd wondered how I looked. I hastily poured myself another gin and tonic, set it down on the table in front of the couch, and excused myself to the restroom.

Flicking on the bathroom light, I moved swiftly to the mirror, examining my face. I rubbed at a brown dot in the corner of my mouth, realizing a few seconds later that it was a freckle. Had that always been there? I supposed it had to have been. My face looked a bit red in the cheeks, so I splashed water on my face as if it'd mute out the color, flushed the toilet, strategically washed my hands, and headed back out.

Sitting down lightly on the couch, I turned to face Frank, who had made no motion to the TV clicker to restart the movie.

"It's a lot to take in, isn't it?"

Although not necessarily a tense movie, we happened to pause the movie after a graphic sex scene. I said I was enjoying the pacing, and asked how he was liking it so far. He mentioned something about the acting, but I was distracted as his knee bumped into mine. It dawned on me that we were both sitting on our respective sides of the sectional, but we were sitting much closer to the connected corner. I let my leg stay where his was.

I shifted my body forward to grab my drink, and took a tiny sip. I was staring straight ahead at the TV in front of us, but I could feel his gaze on my profile. Even without looking, I knew it wasn't his usual entertained astonishment that warranted the majority of his lingering stares. I couldn't place what his face was communicating to me, but it almost seemed like he was choking. Like he was trying to gasp for air. Like he was holding his breath while going through a tunnel.

"Do you want to kiss?"

I furrowed my brow in confusion. Had he really asked me that? I wasn't entirely sure, and I looked over at him, my face still frowning.

"What did you say?"

"Do you want to kiss... me?"

The extra word added for clarification made me feel bad for asking. It'd certainly taken a lot for him to ask me, and I'd given him the added pressure of needing to repeat those words yet again, plus one.

I paused, not stunned, but unsure of how to proceed. I felt as though any verbal confirmation would feel a bit more formal, leading the situation in an even weirder direction.

I pressed both hands down on the couch to lift myself up, and I scooted toward him. I looked at his mouth as I parted mine, and pressed my gin-soaked lips against his. His lips didn't push back at first. They just let me come to him.

I slid my thigh closest to him along the outside of his, and carefully lifted my other thigh slowly upward and over his other leg, straddling him while I parted my lips to nibble on him, moving my face along his neck, breathing gently into his ear. Frank let out a soft grunt, and turned his face toward mine nuzzled in his neck, begging me to come back up to him.

    Our lips met again, and I felt my tongue slowly fill his mouth, and grabbing his face with both of my hands, I sunk deeper into his lap, wheeling my hips, our kissing sporadically punctuated by gentle moans and heavy breathing. I felt my breathing getting louder, more uncontrollable, more arrhythmic. Before I even had time to process what I'd been saying, I heard my quieted voice echo into his mouth.

    "Do you want to go upstairs?"

Walking the Dog

Once things get started, it always feels weird to move to another room or area to keep things moving. Part of me wished I hadn't asked for us to go upstairs, because then it meant me having to dismount him, which was a lot less graceful than when I'd mounted him. There was also the added pressure of how to walk upstairs. Did I run to show how eager I was? Would that be weird and childish? Or were we supposed to keep kissing while moving up toward his bedroom, slowly?

As I stood up, staring down at him, he hadn't made any effort to stand himself up, so I walked slowly to the staircase by myself, placed my hand on the rail, and turned around to look back at him. I gently stroked the handrail with my palm, staring longingly at him, cocking my head to the side inquisitively. Frank finally forced himself up, and with enough of a head start, I slowly walked upstairs as he lagged behind me. I turned the corner to his bedroom, which took up the entirety of the second floor.

His bedroom looked like a stock photo, with soft blues and general neutrals. His décor didn't quite express who he was as a person. I'd half expected eccentric artwork from foreign countries, with zany colors and patterns. Yet, his bedroom was neat, simple.

I'd recalled our email exchanges while he was in Latvia, where I'd been going through a break up with a boyfriend I'd been living with. Upon his moving out, I was able to decorate my room in a manner that reflected me, and only me. I had even sent Frank photos of my room, the weird little kitschy knick knacks and toys I'd thought exemplified me. I had a childlike wonder of my own space, and felt so comfortable sharing it with him.

 It didn't occur to me that months later he, too, would be showing me his bedroom.

I sat on the bed and peered up at him, just as he entered his room. He scanned the room, looking for any embarrassing messes or oversights, and then he sat on the bed next to me. He reached his hand toward me, grabbing the back of my head, and he began to press his face into mine.

His tongue darted around, lapping, and winding around from impossible angles. It was hard for me not to pull away. I felt as though some kind of creature was trying to infiltrate my body, using it as a host for world domination. I tried to dodge his tongue by closing my mouth, but as though unable to show any mercy, it persisted. Its dying wish was to completely drench my mouth in saliva.

I decided to gently push him back, my hand on his chest. He looked at me, bewildered, smiling, as though he'd been doing something well, and that he was expectant of a reward. I used the intermission to remove my jacket, and unbutton my top. As I looked down, I noticed my stomach protruding over my jeans, and immediately felt pudgy and self-conscious, so I decided to find a way to get us to lay down so that my torso could be flat, extended outward. I grabbed him by the shirt and pulled him toward me as I laid myself down with him on top of me.

Pulling on the collar of his shirt, I brought him up toward me. His arms, unwilling to hold himself up, buckled under his weight and he collapsed onto me. The air cooped up in my lungs escaped from me in a sneeze-like fashion. I rolled my body out from under him, pressing him over to one side of me.

I tried to kiss him.

He seemed more interested in feeling the jagged edges of my molars, painting them with his spit.

Frustration overwhelmed me. Things had been going so well downstairs. Things had felt good. Now, I felt as though I were fighting some force, preventing me from making things just so. I kept pressing on his chest, to push him away from me, and each time we stopped kissing he'd look at me expectantly, and when I would go in to kiss him again, his mouth would attack me once more. I wanted to climb on top of him, to guide him, but I was made aware once again of my body, and how I'd wanted it elongated to appear as thin as possible.

For me, intimacy and gentle foreplay didn't last long because I'd always been worried about someone observing my flaws. An undetected black hair under my chin that could be seen only while kissing my neck. A stretch mark on my hips, or cellulite spackling the backs of my thighs. I felt like I was constantly under a microscope, unnoticeable from afar, which is where I usually kept people. But with the proper focus, everything could be seen so vividly, even the parts of myself I wasn't aware of.

As a result, sex was a way to bring people even closer to me, the focus obstructed by its proximity to me, and people were then no longer able to examine me.

A microscope lens pressed too close to the slide of the sample.

The slide shattering what was meant to be observed.

I was so frustrated by my wanting him to let me kiss him, but wanting him to see me and my body in a specific way. I wanted to scream. I decided I could dodge his tongue attacks by taking breaks to remove articles of clothing.

After my jacket and top went my pants. I'd resented the creasing the jeans left indented on my thighs, and in an effort to direct his attention away from my legs, I'd snapped off my bra. I looked up at Frank's face, as he stared longingly at my breasts.

Although my breasts had always been above average for my frame, I'd always been insecure about them. In part because my left breast is noticeably larger than my right breast, but more because of my experiences with doctors during physicals and routine health checkups. They would routinely stare at my nipples with a look of confusion, and ask if they've always looked like that to which I'd reply that I thought so.

To that, they'd ask no further questions or offer any further explanation. I'd never really fully quite known how or why my nipples are a cause for concern, but as a consequence, I'd tried to avoid people staring at them for extended periods of time.

Unless they were doctors.

Although, Frank was technically a doctor.

I was running out of articles of clothing to remove in an effort to avoid Frank's wet daggers, so I decided to start disrobing him. I began to move my face away from his, toward his neck, while unbuttoning his shirt with one hand. I'd known my actions were only telling him that I wanted him, even though I wanted him to stop. I was saying yes in every way imaginable, with no thought toward what that meant for the future.

Finally, as I started undoing his belt, Frank stood up quickly, and quietly moved toward the edge of his bed to stand up and look down at me. I propped myself up on my elbows, subtly flexed my stomach, and looked up at him with a light sense of confusion. I decided to breathe heavily moving my chest to seem like I'd been in the throes of passion instead of avoiding his tongue from inducing my gag reflex.

"I... need a few things."

He maneuvered clunkly to his nightstand and pulled out a small plastic bottle of KY. It took me a few seconds longer than I'd like to admit to process what he'd been doing. I wasn't aware of my face, or whether or not my stomach looked flat, or if my nipples looked weird.

"Also, I don't like condoms."

"It's okay, I'm on birth control."

At that, he unfastened his own belt, removed his jeans, and took off his underwear. He crawled toward me, and rose up above me on his knees. He began stroking his flaccid penis. He paused to add a generous amount of KY jelly to his palm before continuing to coat his penis with the lubricant. I began to reach out to help him stroke himself, but he moved his hips away from me.

"I have to do it myself."

I looked down at his penis, yet saw no discernable differences between each jerk, each glossing of the lube seemed to be doing nothing to engorge him. Still, he continued to reapply more lubricant, adding more and more of the meaningless liquid.

Slathering a hotdog with too much tasteless ketchup.

I still had no idea what I looked like.

Snapping back to focus, I'd decided to help him visually, so I slid my thong off, and started to masturbate in front of him, hoping it'd somehow make him erect. Nothing came of it. I started to slow down, and I was about to ask if something was wrong. He saw I was about to ask a question, so he fumbled on top of me, and slid his jelly slicked fingers inside of me.

He moved his fingers in a circle, painting the walls with a scooping motion, like dipping a chip into a bowl of guacamole, before bringing it up to his mouth. He grabbed his penis, which still didn't look any more interested than it had earlier, and he began to press it into my vagina.

Perhaps once he started to feel my vagina, he would finally get hard and fuck me.

However, with each feeble attempt to lob himself inside of me, he could only barely get in part of his bent shaft before it came blobbing outward again. I'd realized eventually, that what he wanted his penis to do was the same flicking motion, but into me instead of outside of me. I grabbed his wormy member and brought it toward the back of my vagina, flicking it upward.

His penis slid into me in a crane-like movement. I'd felt a strong sense of accomplishment, and even began to moan and breathe heavily in approval of myself. He started to quickly pump himself into me, letting out a yell, then collapsed on top of me.

He came.

Although already completely laid back, I managed to sink down even further in shock.

He rolled over to the side he'd occupied prior to using my body as a parking spot, and looked at me, happily, dopily. I couldn't help but wonder how he could possibly feel proud, or any semblance of pleasure from what just happened. Wasn't he ashamed?

Growing up, my sister and I'd begged my mom for a dog. She obliged, under the condition that we'd have to learn to take care of it, tend to it, and clean up after it. I remember the first time I'd taken our little Bichon named Daisy on a walk, watching her hind legs pump upward toward her front, while she crouched her body into a triangular shape, and she began to take a shit on the sidewalk. I had come prepared, as I promised my mother I would, with a small plastic bag so I could pick up the shit, and throw it away properly.

I'd felt this sense of shame, picking up the fecal matter, which was still warm even through the plastic bag. I felt embarrassed, but couldn't understand why. I looked at Daisy, who even while taking the shit had looked at me blissfully, and was still doing so, her eyes like she'd just taken a bong rip and her mouth stretched into the biggest smile.

As I tied the bag, I couldn't help but think, "okay wait. She just pooped in public. Why does she look so pleased with herself? And why am I the one that's ashamed?"

Busy Summer

My eyes darted away from his and toward his bathroom and I knew I'd found an excuse to leave the bed abruptly. I got up hurriedly, and looking at myself in the mirror, I was greeted with what my face had looked like for the past five minutes.

What I saw was horrifying. My face looked gaunt, scared. I was out of my element, and deeply disappointed. At that moment, I hadn't liked what had happened to me, but I felt as though I was in too deep. I couldn't see a way to get myself out of this hole I'd dug myself into, being so caught up in the moment. I knew I couldn't tell him how despicable that had been, how sad and pathetic, even though I couldn't help but wonder how he didn't know that already.

Was I being too critical, or was he incredibly lacking in self-awareness that I'd assumed most adults had? Or maybe he didn't want to have to talk about it, which was also an understandable possibility. Was I the one who was immature for not being okay with what just happened? I mean, how many 21-year-old women sleep with 43 year olds, thinking the sex would actually be good?

I couldn't decide which one of us was wrong, and I didn't want to spend any more time looking at myself, trying to decide. I realized, no matter which one of us was more in the wrong, I still wasn't proud of myself.

I walked out of the bathroom and plunked down on the bed, bouncing up lightly and giggling at the unexpected lift. Frank looked at me with his same I-just-took-a-shit-and-you-cleaned-it-up look, and I shied away from his eyes. I didn't feel much like talking, and it felt too weird to leave. I closed my eyes and said nothing. I had been perfectly content just lying there in silence, with my eyes closed.

My solace was broken suddenly, Frank miraculously making the situation more awkward.

"So, are you excited for graduation next week?"

I shuddered. I hadn't really told him about my reservations, about how I didn't feel like the ceremony was all that important to me, that I'd had a recent disagreement with my mom, which was really just me being angry at her and her playing dumb. My step dad, naturally, defended her baselessly.

I hadn't meant not walking for graduation as a punishment, but more of a decision based on whether or not it was actually something I personally wanted to do. Not only did I want to avoid bringing up something that would make me seem inferior, pedantic—I'm fighting with my mommy so I'm throwing a fit—but I didn't really want to think about him seeing me at graduation, the disparity between us, the pretending like he didn't empty himself inside of me.

"I'm a bit on the fence about it, actually. I'm considering not walking, just because I don't really see the importance of the ceremonial aspect of it."

I thought it was an articulate cover up.

"Well, sure, most of the theatrics are asinine, but it's a once in a lifetime experience. It's long, boring, and the speeches are generally uninteresting, but it's a special moment. You should definitely walk."

I sighed, and deep down, I supposed he had a point, but there was also a sense of pride I'd felt when I hadn't done something that others had. The same way I think myself better than others for only having spent fifteen minutes at prom, and I didn't even have my photo taken. Or when I tell people I've never had a Big Mac, or a Twinkie, I get far more enjoyment from people's reactions to my presumed uniqueness than I would from actually having participated in any of those events.

"Well, maybe. I've got the robes. I'm still thinking about it."

Upon continuing the conversation, I asked if he'd be attending the ceremony, and what that would be like for him.

"Oh, it's goofy. We have to wear these ridiculous hats. But it's all in good fun. Really, you should go."

I wasn't quite sure why he was so hell bent on me attending, but decided he'd just really thought that all students should attend ceremonies of accomplishment. I shrugged and turned my body upward, so that I was flat on my back, staring up at the ceiling.

"You know, I wasn't planning on any of this. At least, not prior to me planning my summer, and, well, I've got a lot of things scheduled. As you know, I'm leaving for Seoul in two weeks."

I continued to stare up at the ceiling in a distracted way, and couldn't help but wonder which of one of two things he was getting at. I'd made an outcome line plot on the ceiling above me, starting first with his comment. This meant he was trying to communicate one of two things: he was trying to let me down easy and explain that he wouldn't have time to be with me anymore. I was okay with this. The other option was he was insinuating that this was more than a one night stand, and we'd needed to discuss it further. I didn't know how I felt about that.

Stunned, I'd realized I hadn't even thought that far ahead. If he were trying to let me down easy, then the next outcome would suggest I need not say or do anything. I liked that route. However, considering the other fork, that he'd expected more and we'd need to discuss further... that I wasn't quite sure how to tackle. In my experience, if I have sex with someone, we usually don't discuss anything further until three months or so down the line, or never at all, leaving the conversation and texts to slowly taper off.

"Yeah, I know, you told me. That's really okay."

I almost just assumed it was a one night stand, or at least something meant to be incredibly short, fleeting. Nothing that required much more discussion or planning, especially after the flaccid flopping fiasco.

He'd gone on to discuss many of his other adventures for the summer, how he'd be going to Michigan for a month, as he'd been awarded a grant to study at a university library, followed by a literary conference in Austria in which he would be presenting an essay related to the theme of that year's seminar. He would also plan on visiting his family in California toward the end of summer, before returning back for the start of the new school year.

"huh, South Korea, Michigan, Austria, and California... that does sound like quite a hectic summer."

My response felt robotic.

"Yeah! It's always so exciting. Oh! And I'm also running these two summer programs at school, one of which…"

His voice trailed off in my head as I began to slowly lose interest in his excitement. I'd always felt very strange when people started talking about their plans, or successes, as I'd felt it had always bordered on bragging. How could that be a conversation?

I'd found that when I talked to people entirely full of themselves, bragging or talking about something that couldn't be a back and forth, that always left the listener in a position to nod and give blasé answers like "Oh, that's nice," and "Cool," or could only ask questions in response, keeping the conversation tipped in the braggart's favor.

Since high school, whenever I suspected someone about to go on a long-winded monologue about how awesome they were, I tended to tune them out entirely. It was far more fun for me to choose when my mind would snap back to reality and pick up on some of their last words, using tonal and fluctuation clues to determine when I thought they'd be wrapping up what they'd been going on about. I'd then pick out some of the words I could retrieve from my memory and piece together some meaningless sentence in accordance with their brags, they'd seem thrilled, and moved on, and I'd have a secret that I was never really listening or caring.

The world would keep turning, and I wouldn't go postal. It was my own little secret in how I'd been able to keep the peace and maneuver through conversations with people I didn't care about, detached but appearing present. Getting away with this gave me more pleasure than any inane conversation ever could.

I was always confused by this common human need to talk about oneself at length. Was it for validation? Or was that just... how people talked? I never really said anything about myself unless I was drunk, or if someone asked me directly, or unless I had wanted advice or suggestions. I had generally seen no point in talking about myself. I'd been in groups of people, talking about anime and TV shows they liked, while I stood off to the side, confused as to why anyone would want to discuss something unless they had questions, or anything was up for debate.

"Oh, and the part where he beat the bad guy? Incredible."

"Yes! Agreed, and the sidekick? So funny!"

I'd turned away from people, these excessive exchanges. They always reminded me of children, and I'd felt like any sort of conjecture I'd add to the conversation would quite similarly be like a kid telling their tired parents about their day on the ride home from school.

"And then, we had pizza for lunch!"

"Uh-huh"

"And then Timmy got chocolate milk instead of regular milk because he found an extra quarter before school!"

"You don't say."

"And then, Mrs. Sparkle let us color for five extra minutes today."

"No kidding."

I'd craved chaos, and a twist. Tell me something. Did you find a severed finger on your pizza? Did Timmy, in fact, steal the quarter from the school bully, who'd proceeded to beat him up? Did Mrs. Sparkle let you color extra today because she's going through a divorce and is slowly losing interest in her daily life?

No arguments, nothing thought provoking, no conflict.
I didn't see the point.

Part of me did believe that it was a totally normal human thing to want, to do, to relate to people in some way. I'd understood my inability, or the strained ability, made me the odd one. I couldn't help but wonder what made people feel this urge to share? Was it that everyone thought they were interesting, unique, and special?

Did I find myself especially uninteresting, and felt uncomfortable talking about myself? Was I ashamed of myself? The constant "I don't knows" and shrugging people off was perhaps finally getting to me.

This was one of those moments in which I was completely detached from what he was saying, but part of me was also incredibly jealous. All that travel, all those experiences he was going to have, certainly, he'd earned them. I hadn't.

Yet, I'd wanted them badly. I wanted to seek the unknown, travel, live life, but I was about to graduate and had no job lined up, had only started considering graduate school in an effort to push off the impending doom of not knowing what to do after graduation with a degree in Mathematics. I'd felt a sense of "what now?" that all adults told me they'd kill for.

"Enjoy that time! Explore! Find yourself!"

It all felt so meaningful, yet so out of reach. It almost felt menacing to listen to people offer me options that I knew I couldn't have.

I knew Frank had worked hard to be where he was in life, and although not bitter, I was envious. I'd wanted offers to be whisked away to Austria. I wanted to have close ties with universities in South Korea.

Perhaps the Michigan thing I could live without, but there was something romantic about spending a month plunging into books in a special section of a world-famous library.

My head swirled with thoughts of me, traveling, sought after. In a never-ending whirlwind of being wanted, important, having opportunities abound for me to go everywhere, eat anything, do everything.

For me, I knew it was never anyone else I wanted to connect with, but the world I wanted to be a part of. A world that was only slightly touched and explored, but still mostly a stranger to me. Perhaps, I'd never wanted anyone else's validation, but my own, and whatever else was out there.

Two of Swords

We awoke the next morning, still unclothed, on the furthest ends of the bed. Frank had been snoring lightly, which was actually quite comforting. I knew that there were definitely times when I would snore, especially if I'd consumed alcohol, so if my counterpart was snoring, I felt like that was one less flaw he'd notice about me.

I delicately rolled out of bed, and walked back to the restroom attached to his bedroom. I stared at myself in the mirror, my hair bouncy and blown out, and I'd realized how good I'd felt. I looked good. I glanced outside the door at Frank, still sleeping awkwardly in his bed, and couldn't quite remember what had actually been so bad about last night.

The first time you have sex with anyone, it's usually a bit fumbly and weird. Both people are still trying to figure each other out, not quite wanting to overstep, or be too demanding, or present anything too weird or kinky at first.

Plus, he's old. I don't think he's been having a lot of sex recently, so he's probably out of practice. Once we get things going at a regular pace, I'm sure it'll get better.

*She **Lies** Still*

I caught myself, realizing that I had been planning for things to move forward. Last night, that was the furthest thing from my mind, yet now, I was hoping that things would continue, and expected them to only get better. It was as though I didn't want to leave it at that, because it had been so subpar, so unsatisfactory. It was the same logic I'd used if I had been dumped, and heartbroken, only to have my ex come crawling back so that I could tell him to fuck off. I'd wanted to eventually edge him out, to have the upperhand.

At this point, I'd felt like I was below net-neutral, and he was well positive above that line. I'd needed the scales tipped in my favor, and I hadn't yet determined how I was going to do that.

Taking one last look at my reflection, I tossed my hair back and crawled back into bed. It dawned on me that I had an engagement—the newspaper end of the year retreat at the lake house owned by the catholic monks of the university—and it was my duty to pick up drinks and some of the staff members that didn't have cars. As this wasn't a completely stiff morning after goodbye, I felt no qualms poking Frank awake, to tell him I needed to get going. I was completely unaware of the time, and in no particular rush, but I felt as though I needed some sort of way to command my wanting to leave. I poked the sleeping bear.

Frank stirred, and looked a bit startled to see me at first, as though he'd forgotten about the night before. His eyes relaxed as he gazed up and down my body, settling on my face, beaming up at me.

"I have to get going... I have that retreat to go to. I've got errands to run, and people to round up."

Frank stretched and let out a morning groan, turning his face back toward me.

"Right, that's at around noon though, isn't it?"

How did he know what time the retreat was? I gave him a curious look.

"Yeah, I'm actually going to that as well, just to show face. I'm actually on the board."

I had known this, and although he'd always been the type of professor to go above and beyond, ensuring the best for the students, it hadn't occurred to me in the slightest that he'd actually be attending. It was just going to be students and the faculty advisor overseeing that we didn't destroy the lake house.

I realized I wouldn't be able to let loose as I'd liked to at this event. I couldn't help but think that there'd be, in a sense, two babysitters watching the children in their playpen, ensuring as little destruction as possible until their mommies and daddies were ready to pick them up. I'd been looking forward to joking around with some friends, feeling the last semblance of childlike fun before graduation.

Granted, Frank hadn't put this pressure on me, but I wanted him to still see me as someone set apart from the rest. Mature, stately, and as managing editor—albeit not editor-in-chief—I'd wanted to show that I was, in fact, able to oversee things just as the adults could. I wanted a seat at the big kid's table.

"I actually made a blueberry banana bread for the party! Want to see?"

I smiled generously at his excitement, and nodded politely. I stood up and began to dress, my eyes darting across the floor to find my scattered articles of clothing. I didn't really remember having thrown them as far across the room as they were, but I found myself searching for Easter eggs while Frank stared at me, a proud parent watching his baby girl find everything he'd hidden.

Walking downstairs, I immediately saw the pillows askew on the sectional, where things had started so well. The TV had dimmed after hours of neglect, and Frank grabbed the clicker to relieve it of its last efforts. I swooped up the glasses barely touched from the night before, and brought them to the kitchen, setting them down in the sink. I turned around and lifted the mojito up in an offering to Frank, who smiled and shook his head animatedly. I cocked my head in a "suit yourself" manner, and lifted the drink up to my lips, taking a small sip for the desired effects. His eyes lit up and he let out a hearty laugh, while my insides flooded with heat and ease.

I dumped the rest of the drink into the sink, and walked over to him. He removed two small pans of banana bread from the refrigerator, one in each hand, and presented them to me. He beamed at them, looking so proud of his creations, and I found myself forced to acknowledge his delicious looking breads. He offered me a piece, but I'd declined in an effort to not overstay my own standard of the welcome. Frank looked a bit hurt, his arms drooping slightly.

"I'll have some later, at the lake house?" I added, reassuringly.

This perked him up, and I began to walk past him. We stood shoulder to shoulder, and I looked up at his face.

Should I kiss him goodbye? I couldn't necessarily hug him, could I? His hands were full. I couldn't just leave, right?

Surprisingly, I found myself not wanting to. I actually wanted to embrace him, and I didn't fully understand why. Hadn't I just been embarrassed by him? Hadn't I felt like a five-year-old, holding a stinking, warm bag of his shit? Yet, I wanted to hold him, and for what reason? I couldn't quite decide. Was it to console him, or was it me who needed consoling?

I'd held out my arms, cocking my head jokingly to see if he'd take the bait. He did a sort of laughing bow, both of his hands full, and grabbed me, crossing both banana bread pans behind my back. I buried my face into his chest, imagining the two of swords tarot card. A person crossing two swords in front of themselves, eyes covered in a sash.

My shoulders slumped, face burrowed into Frank's chest, I knew I was the one wearing the blindfold.

The Lake House

Rounding up the younger news staff members from campus, we began our modest voyage to the lake house. The excitement buzzing in my little sedan made me feel as though my position in life was seemingly unchanged. I was chatting with 20 year olds, and felt a sense of belonging. I had been the only one about to graduate, though, and even though the way they spoke to me relayed that they viewed me as different, other, I knew this was the only sense of normalcy I'd felt in the most recent weeks.

This was as close as I could feel to inclusion, my choices throughout my life making that feeling more and more foreign to me.

I was unfamiliar with the route, but one of the section editors was on map duty. He'd been there the year before and I had declined in an effort to not be part of the team. He was guiding us in a way I wouldn't have been able to.

Prior to my first year at university, I had gotten a job working in catering. I thought it'd be convenient, and the odd hours would be a good way to stagger work and money into my university schedule. Upon starting, I noticed my manager hadn't scheduled me at all during the orientation weekend, and when I inquired as to why, he looked at me furiously and said so I could participate in the orientation, instead of working at it.

I stared at the paper schedule posted in the noisy kitchen, hearing the clangs and shouts of pans and chefs, respectively, and I turned to look at my manager again and said I'd rather just work than have to deal with all that first-year orientation stuff.

He promptly penciled me into each lunch and dinner event.

This wasn't to say I didn't want any friends. I just knew that the initial meeting, the getting-to-know-you chaos was all bullshit. I didn't want to meet people that way, and there was no appeal in feigning interest with people I didn't care about. Moving into the dorms, the resident assistant for my floor had us all come out of our rooms, and pile into the common area for us to introduce ourselves by saying our names, our majors, and the longest car ride we've ever been on. At the time, I had only been in a car for 6 hours, which sparked a load of chatter.

One student shot a look back at me, eyes wide, and she looked at the student next to her.

"Wow! Only six hours? That sounds great. I wish that was the longest I'd been in a car..." to which her equally dull neighbor agreed, "yeah, that's crazy! I can't imagine being in a car for only six hours!"

How can one not imagine being in a car for only six hours, if they'd been in a car for longer?

Also, why were they talking amongst themselves? Why didn't they talk to me?

I let out an audible sigh, to which both people turned to look at me and turned back around to face the resident assistant again.

After my introduction, I immediately stood up and walked back to my room, completely bored out of my mind by our initial meeting. I was the first person to introduce themselves. I didn't meet anyone else.

The bumpy gravel road that required a concentration reserved for only the most unpleasant activities eventually led to a gorgeous lake house. I wished I'd been able to take advantage it of more than just this once.

The house was perched on the edge of a small cliff, which had rickety stairs leading down to the lake. The grey water looked like it was almost spongy, contrasting with the sharp, jagged shore composed of rocks. It was like a painting by a skilled artist able to use the same colors while creating different textures. It gave me an eerie, early morning feeling that I actually found quite romantic.

We worked our way back up the stairs, praying each step wouldn't give out under our weight, and we went back to my car to unload the drinks and snacks. We started setting things up on the counter, shooting jokes at each other, cracking open beers. Motheringly, I said that I'd let them drink, but they couldn't have more than one. I'd be watching them. They rolled their eyes at me, we cheersed, and everyone sat on the couch and began to joke around.

I found myself arranging and rearranging everything on the counter. We'd bought a lot of snacks, mainly potato chips and junk foods that are easy to absent-mindedly shovel into your mouth while socializing. I knew the advisor would be bringing pizza, so I made sure to clear enough space for that. We could stack the pizza boxes if she decided to bring more than one.

Then I remembered: the banana bread. Would he be bringing both pans, or just the one? How much space should I leave for both the banana breads? I imagined the advisor coming before Frank, and utilizing the extra space I'd left for the banana bread, not realizing how much thought I'd put into the spacing of all the food on the counter. I didn't want all of my efforts to go to waste by having another person rearrange everything, so I decided to hang by the counter, in the kitchen area, while everyone settled in the living room.

Everyone hollered at me from the couches, asking me to join them, but I couldn't seem to leave my nook, holed up in the kitchen, unable to drag myself away and join the others.

"I'm fine here!" I assured them, and I lifted my beer in a salute to them.

They shook their heads and kept on about their business, keeping me in the conversation while I called back out to them, still very much involved, from the outside. I acted coolly, making sure they thought I could join them at any point in time. Little did they know that I was stuck, glued to that kitchen.

Everything needed to be perfect. I was going to see it through.

To my great relief, Edna, the newspaper advisor arrived first, carrying a stack of pizzas that was far more than any of us could finish, and I quickly grabbed the boxes from her, which appeared as an attempt to relieve her from the burden. I didn't think it was obvious that the boxes would be placed exactly where I'd planned for them to be, leaving enough room for the banana bread.

Edna asked how the drive was, what we've been up to so far, and I boasted that I was taking very good care of things, and everyone. Edna seemed resigned to the fact that I hadn't quite joined in on the festivities with everyone, as she'd hoped I would. Edna began busying herself in the kitchenette as well, perusing the refrigerator, giving me sideways glances to see just what I was doing, and what I found so magnetic about standing in the kitchen. I started to recognize I was being watched, observed, and began to fidget, and open one of the bags of potato chips that I didn't even want to eat, while piling a handful onto a paper plate.

I slowly began to munch on a single chip, chewing it far too many times before swallowing the salt and vinegar paste. I found myself staring outside of the sliver of a lateral window from the kitchen, wondering what it was I found so interesting about the gravel parking lot. I looked toward the picture window to my left, with the amazingly dreary view of the lake down below.

I figured it must have seemed strange to the observer, to see me staring outside of the small, meaningless window, in anticipation for nothing in particular. There was something far more spectacular to look at elsewhere.

How strange it was that I wasn't joining my peers on the couch, far more comfortable than leaning against the kitchen counter, enjoying conversations far more lighthearted and meaningful than the one that was currently going on in my head.

Seeing a blue hatchback pull out from the prison tray-sized window, I straightened my posture, and my eyes lit up. I felt myself needing to look to Edna that I hadn't been waiting for that exact moment, and I turned around all too fast, and looked down at another unopened bag of chips, tore at it frantically, dumping more onto my plate.

Edna stared at me, and after a few moments laughed. I realized how ravenous I must have seemed, and I moved over to the boxes of pizzas she'd brought. Why hadn't I just grabbed some pizza? That would have made more sense than filling up on potato chips. I shoved the mountain of chips to one side of my plate and opened the top box, and grabbed whatever pizza was there, lopping it onto my plate.

I glanced up at Edna, who was still staring at me curiously. I greeted her with a smile, as though I hadn't noticed that her eyes hadn't left me since she'd arrived, and lifted the plate up in a sort of acknowledgement while thanking her for bringing the pizza. Her gaze seemed to soften, and as soon as I'd felt her skepticism ease, the front door clicked. I whipped around, expectant but somehow startled by Frank's entrance. Frank, one hand lingering on the door knob, the other occupied with one pan of banana bread, paused to glance between Edna and I, his face unreadable.

"Why, hello!"

Frank's booming greeting was the perfect opportunity to take a small bite of the pizza. Lifting the piece to my mouth with one hand, while squeezing out a casual "hi" with my teeth clenched over the pizza. I used my other hand to scoot the pizza boxes over a bit, motioning to the area I'd reserved for his banana bread. He immediately picked up on my obscene gesticulations and slid the pan alongside the pizza boxes, his forearm grazing mine in the process.

I chose not to make eye contact, instead choosing to look up at Edna, who seemed to have decided that my repulsive greeting toward Frank was enough of my face she'd wanted to see for the day, and she fidgeted weirdly in the refrigerator, pulling out some beer and offered one to Frank. Obliging, he took one, raised his glass to cheers me, and I nudged my paper plate into his beer. As he took a corner, I remained leaning against the counter.

I'd felt satisfied that all the snacks and food had fit on the counter space, and although my job was essentially finished, a huge weight lifted off of my shoulders, I still felt I couldn't join everyone on the couches. Granted, some of them had gone down to the lake, but as for the rest, I couldn't bring myself to sit with them. I still felt tethered to the counter, unable to feel as though I could enter the bubble around everyone.

Part of me was worried that Edna would see that I had waited until now, until Frank had arrived, to then join everyone. I felt that in and of itself seemed suspicious, so I decided to continue to post up by the counter, as though this was where I'd planned on hanging for the entirety of the party. Another part of me felt as though I actually would be interrupting something socially.

The excited chatter that was punctuated by bursts of laughter made me feel as though I could never jump in at the right moment without ruining the bond already formed within the people who'd already planted themselves there. Sure, some people had moseyed off and started doing something new, but I felt leaving the group was much easier than joining an already formed group.

I sighed and bent forward, adjusting my lower back to fit underneath the ledge of the counter. Frank had positioned himself near the picture window, overlooking the lake. With the grey light shining through, the vision of the back of his outline appeared black, and for a moment, he was a model in a black and white postcard, staring out, bottle of beer in one hand.

I took a mental photo, and thought about all of the ways I would have perfected the scene. He was hunched over in a way that made him appear to have no neck. I wanted to go up to him, push gently on his upper back while pressing his shoulders back, to straighten him up. This would make his stature a more erect presence, and the longer neck would amplify how I thought his head should be angled.

I would have had him tilt his head three quarters, to catch the side of his profile, and instruct him to lift the beer bottle carefully up to his lips, like he was taking a swig.

Or maybe, no, I wanted him to be clutching it while staring off into the distance, deep in thought, but clearly still drinking while doing so. Maybe I just wanted him to have it lifted, as though he were trying to blow on the opening, to make a hollow whistling sound.

Yeah, that was what I wanted.

The intensity in the eyes, but with the bottle as a useful prop.

And the grey. I wanted the grey.

There, I thought. Perfect.

Bear and Bull

"You were supposed to call me last night, you freak. Tell me everything."

The next day, I'd hastily called my sister, forgetting that I'd told her I'd call her the night prior. She had known I had gone to Dr. Joyce's house, and that I'd had before, and she was vocal about her lack of approval. Chloe had also gone to the same university, graduating three years before me, and was familiar with Dr. Joyce as well.

"Well, I mean, that's. There's. I mean, I stayed the night. You can guess what happened. Your guess would probably be true. There's not much to tell."

She sighed audibly over the phone. "Look, it's weird. He's your professor..."

I quickly interjected to defend myself.

"Well, not for much longer, and I was never an English major, and it's not like I was doing it for a grade, or that I expect any preferential treatment because I'm not currently enrolled in any of his classes."

"Hold on, I wasn't finished," Chloe interrupted.

"Don't jump down my throat. He's your professor, but. I get it. He's hot. That's hot."

Despite our obvious differences, Chloe and I always got along famously, and she's the one person's opinion I really, truly value. The funny thing about being sisters—and I've heard the same goes for brothers—is that there's an endless stream of comparisons, and unwarranted and crass comments. There'd been countless scenarios where we'd introduce one another to friends, acquaintances, and instead of a "Nice to meet you" or an extended hand, we'd hear, "Oh! You're prettier than she is!"

That never worked just one way. It was as though being a sibling of the same gender gave the world an open invitation to compare, to judge, and so unabashedly so that they'd tell you openly, to your face, that one was hotter, skinner, more or less something than the other. My sister and I faced this from a young age, but we'd always brush it off. We never held it against the other, knowing that people were completely unaware of how insulting and entitled they were to their opinions. What they were hoping to achieve with those comments was always beyond and beneath us.

I'd even asked someone once what made them feel it was necessary to blurt out such a rude observation, to which they shrugged and laughed.

I'd eventually come to the conclusion that people don't ever think about the repercussions of their thoughts, or actions.

People just like talking.

"But, you know. It is still weird, dude."

One specific difference my sister and I have is how we relate to authority figures. Though we both like to be on a closer, more chummy level with them, our motives couldn't be more different. My sister loved academia, and she enjoyed working closely with professors and teachers, showcasing her talents and asking deeper questions, understanding as much as humanly possible, and then some. Not only did she enjoy knowledge, and learning, and being able to prove that she is far more intelligent than most, but I do believe she also loved when people of academic and intellectual esteem regarded her in the same way. As equals.

I admired her for her ability to work in close, respectable proximity to these influential people twice her senior, and for her to be seen as a true equal amongst them.

I, on the other hand, had a love-hate relationship with authority. I never respected authority by legitimate means as a title, or label. Respect, to me, must be earned through reference. My overall wanting to befriend teachers and professors throughout my life was more of a middle finger to the system. I wanted to show myself and others that labels and positions of power would buckle under my weight, if I so wanted them to. It was less about intellectual prowess for me, and more about showing myself as an equal by snaking and weaseling, and saddling up next to them. Not to achieve anything out of them, per say, but for myself to know that I was somehow equal to them.

"Yeah, I get that. It's weird," I responded genuinely. "It wasn't something we'd been planning, and it kind of just happened. I don't know, maybe it'd been escalating for a while and I just hadn't realized it."

Chloe sensed the hesitation in my voice, a sense of confusion, and maybe even a slight need for her validation.

"Look, I knew you'd changed a lot since your last relationship. It was three years, and you've been very anti-commitment for a while now. I knew it'd take someone special to change that for you. I think he's a special person. He's smart, articulate, interesting. If this is something you think you're going to pursue, I support you."

Again, I hadn't thought far enough ahead after the one night stand. I still hadn't even asked to think what he'd wanted, but I figured I'd just go along for the ride.

Then, Chloe spat out loudly over the phone, "So, how was it?!"

Fuck, after she said it was hot, after she said he was hot, I didn't want to be honest with how disappointing the sex had been.

But now, maybe I'd be dating a professor. We'd have intimate conversations, a meeting of the minds… maybe. Sex would just be a thing we'd do here or there, and it wouldn't matter how satisfying it was because everything else would be mind-blowing.

Or maybe dating someone older was the same as dating someone my age. There were no secret tricks he'd pull out from summers abroad, or no cool tips he'd have for me from a conference across the country.

Maybe with people, what you see is what you get.

I'm no different. Although, with me, it's more of what I show you is what you get.

"Cathy?"

"It was fine." I pretended that being lost in thought was a consequence of me thinking about how great the sex had been. I giggled.

Later that evening, I met up with my friend Chase at a seedy dive bar located between both of our cities. He was two years older than me, and one of my best friends and confidants. The type of person who will tell you everything like it is to your face, be honest and upfront with you, make fun of you relentlessly, and who'd confide his deepest secrets to you as well, so you'd never feel alone swimming in your own pool of doubt and errors.

There was this sense that, because of our shared interests in strange-doings, we did enable each other quite a bit, however, we were as thick as thieves, and nothing could really break that kind of bond.

After ordering our beers, we slid into our respective wooden benches and began catching up. As per usual, I'd asked him about his girlfriend at the time, to which he divulged a charming story about how they'd been making out, and how she'd discovered a receipt in his pocket, and without any consideration of his past exploits, or things he'd potentially hidden from her, when she inquired as to the unmarked receipt, with an address printed on it, even Chase's curiosity had gotten the best of him. They both decided to search the address to determine where the receipt had come from. As it turned out, it had been from a strip club, which his girlfriend had repeatedly voiced her disdain for, and to which he'd perpetually denied attending.

Chase didn't have the same fascination with strip clubs that I did. His interests were mainly social. His guy friends and co-workers would want to go, so he'd attend without much resistance. He'd always wanted to be in his girlfriends' good graces, and always hid and lied about his transgressions in order to save face. Although it was something I'd always made fun of him for, his girlfriends never wanted to meet me, or be friends with me. I figured, I'd been given an out for the responsibility to be honest with them. I wasn't going to try too hard to be noble.

"And they were really thorough... The server's name on the receipt was CARL. Fucking Carl, there was no fucking Carl there. The server was also a stripper. Fucking bullshit." Chase groaned.

"Well, dude, if you knew you were doing something wrong, you definitely should have been more careful. The way I see it, you have three options. You can just be honest about what you want. When guy friends ask you to go, and you know your girlfriend will be upset and say no, then you'll have to face their scrutiny, but if you're truly happy about it, it really won't matter in the long run. If you really do want to go to the strip club, I suggest being up front with your girlfriend from the beginning. If they don't agree with an aspect of your lifestyle, that's a huge red flag for both of you in the future. Or, if you wanna sneak around, you just have to be better about keeping your secrets. Can't be too sloppy or careless."

Chase let out a guffaw.

"Nice life advice. I either have to disappoint at least one person, or get better at being bad. Great. Can't wait to hear what you've been up to."

■ ■ ■

Upon hearing about my recent escapades, Chase's mouth seemed incapable of closing. He glared at me, almost angrily, as though I'd said something insulting to him.

"You're fucking joking. What are we talking, here? I'm imagining tweed jackets, tortoise shell glasses. Cigar?"

I shook my head and giggled. "Far from it."

More often than not, Frank wore Hawaiian shirts, a nod to growing up in California, while also thwarting the idea of formal or business casual dress. He'd pair them with jeans, a light blue color that seemed to suggest a non-decision, a base color of denim. His shoes, sometimes tattered tennis shoes, sometimes creased dress shoes, were either the worst or best parts of his outfit, depending on the day. His hair was completely white, something a bit premature even for his age, and his hairline seemed to be receding in a fashion that reminded me of a shore break ebbing back toward its home in the ocean.

"And he asked if he could kiss you? That's lame. Who asks to kiss someone? You're just supposed to feel it out, and go for it."

At this, I disagreed. Granted, no one had ever asked me to kiss them before, and although it caught me off guard, I wasn't sure which I would have actually preferred. There was a lurching feeling in my chest when Frank had asked me, and it actually excited me to sit with those words. I imagined all the times people just went for it, and kissed me, and although those experiences were pleasant overall, it all had happened so fast that I hadn't actually felt the anticipation that comes with awaiting something truly exhilarating.

"Hello? Where'd you go? Okay, so, he's pretty old, huh? What's that like? How's the sex?"

I'd felt a little unnerved that I'd completely zoned out in front of Chase, although he seemed unbothered, as he was used to it by this point. I thought I'd been responding to his comment, yet I'd just been in my head, having a conversation with myself.

More than his concern or irritation that I went away, he wanted more details about what went down between Frank and me. I divulged everything, honestly, in an effort to make up for my indefinite silence.

Chase and I shared an uncomfortable amount of information with each other, and I'd cackled as I told him about the sex. We'd both completely lost our minds, laughing, crying, and choking.

"Damn, did he need a warm glass of milk after that?" Chase taunted.

I gently placed my head on the table and pretended to slam my head repeatedly, as though tortured with the memories. After the laughter subsided, Chase circled the conversation back to his strip club experience, feeling far more comfortable being open with me after hearing about my debauchery.

"Okay, so honestly, it wasn't JUST that. So the stripper I'd gotten a lap dance from, she somehow slid my semi-erect penis inside of her while she was giving me a dance. Like, she unzipped my pants while I was distracted, and she just popped me right into her for a little bit. Then, she charged me $300 and threatened to call the bouncer over unless I paid her."

I stared at Chase. It was now my turn to be slack-jawed, my mouth hung open, and let out a coughing laugh. I hadn't fully processed what he'd said to me.

"So, you basically cheated on Beth."

Chase, looking down dejectedly, hesitated. "I mean, I didn't want to. I didn't mean to."

Upon realizing how slowly I'd processed the information, I cut him off.

"Wait, you're right. You totally didn't. She, I mean, she raped you. She basically. That's rape. Are you okay? Holy shit man."

I considered this, realizing that Chase hadn't actually consented to anything, and therefore hadn't technically done anything wrong, and that actually something had been done to him. Every comment or question that popped into my head sounded depressingly familiar.

"Well, if you only hadn't been there..." or even "what were you wearing?" I cringed at myself, the questions my mind went to. I also just wanted to know what kind of pants he was wearing, just out of curiosity of the mechanics of how she'd unzipped his pants without him noticing.

"Besides," he chirped, "Beth thinks that anything less than three pumps doesn't count as sex."

Stunned, I allowed my thoughts to be interrupted. I asked for clarification.

"Well, she told me she's only had sex with two other guys. Beth said she's let guys put their penises inside, but her and her sister have a rule that as long as there's fewer than three ins and outs, it doesn't count as sex. So, she's only had sex with two guys, plus me."

"She just wants to keep her number low so people don't think less of her," I said, exasperated, but confused as to why Chase was giving into this logic so easily.

"Well, so, I guess I'm just going to use that little rule so that I don't have to feel as guilty about what happened. I mean, fuck, she's already furious. I don't need that added to the laundry list of my fuck-ups."

I nodded, choosing never to uproot someone's very reasonable coping mechanism.

Although I was never one to lie about the number of people I'd had sex with, I was inclined to lie about whether or not I was having sex with someone. I'd loved having a dirty little secret, and thus, the friend with benefits, or the random hook up always seemed more appealing to me than having an actual long term partner.

What kind of guy would agree to sex with the caveat of only being able to thrust in and out three times, and then be satisfied enough by that?

But then again, why was I so quick to judge?

If Beth wanted to have sex with her friends, but only count a few thrusts before making them stop? If Chase wanted to use that same logic to not feel weird about what happened at the strip club? If I wanted me sleeping with my professor not to be such a big deal, then who was to stop us?

If we decide to add it to the notches on our belts or not, increase our body counts, I suppose that is up to us as individuals. At the end of the day, though, we had just been three people who'd had three pumps, or less. If we didn't think there was anything weird about it, who was anyone else to tell us otherwise?

Picture Day

"So, have you decided?"

"Yeah, I guess I'll walk."

After another week of deliberation, I'd finally decided to walk for graduation, and although I was perfectly satisfied with receiving my expensive piece of paper in the mail, I understood that these types of ceremonies are never for the recipients, but for the guests. From weddings, to graduations, there were very few gatherings where the persons being celebrated actually got to enjoy whatever the celebration was.

"Well, I guess I'll just be seeing you in a bit, then."

The night before graduation, I stayed over at Frank's place, the night itself a blur. I still wasn't sure how I felt about him. When I was with him, I wanted nothing more than to get away, to scream, to hide, to scrape the endless inches of lube off of me, but when I was alone, I couldn't stop thinking about him.

The sex hadn't improved, but things started feeling much more real, much more serious, and I felt a sense of obligation to continue things for as long as he'd wanted. I was always hoping he'd end it, he'd make another passive comment about being strapped for time this summer, so I could catch the hint and move on. It never came. I'd found myself drawn to him while away, revolted by him while with him. I couldn't make up my mind about what I wanted, and I thought about how much easier it'd be if he'd just make the decision for me.

But, he didn't.

"Yeah, I should probably head out."

"Do you want to shower first?"

Yes. "No, I'll be fine."

I gathered my belongings that I'd neatly laid out next to the bed, the night before being far more calculated than the first time, despite nearly everything not going to plan yet again, and I headed downstairs, almost at a gallop toward his front door.

"Wait! CCC."

I paused, and without turning around, I dropped my arm so he'd know I heard him and was awaiting his thought.

"Did I ever tell you that I think you're beautiful?"

I frowned at these words. Too forced. Childly romantic. I found myself so easily doubting him. I felt furious, and although I wanted to turn around and garishly roll my eyes and laugh, I knew I was too angry to have any control over my facial expressions. I lifted my hand up toward the door knob again, and while opening the door, I spun myself outside. I was able to knock the frown off my face for a second before saying "Please don't say that."

The door closing quickly behind me blocked Frank from my blurred vision, and I slammed the door, greeted by the outside sunshine.

Upon lining up in front of the main staircase of Old Main, I'd found some familiar faces to line up with. The warmth of the sun beating down on us, I'd wondered who this procession would actually be benefitting. I remembered my sister's graduation, and how there'd been a Catholic nun giving the dullest welcoming speech. This followed by the Valedictorian, who'd also given the most vanilla, predictable speech that only inspired me to fall asleep, my head rested without consent on the shoulder of the person next to me.

While I was baking outside, my loved ones waited in the auditorium, bored to oblivion, and felt even more emboldened to my negativity, knowing that this couldn't possibly be enjoyable for anyone.

Our coiled line finally started moving, and I marched along with my peers, thrilled to finally be getting things moving. The ceremony went by far quicker than I'd imagined, and I couldn't have been more relieved to be outside, in the open. I found myself under a tent, and spoke to a few of the mathematics professors before having Chloe run up to me, hugging me from behind. My advisor introduced herself to my sister, her eyes never leaving Chloe's face during the entire interaction.

I could tell that my advisor was a little jealous, as Chloe had had her senior thesis published in an academic journal a few years ago. Most professors knew of her. I could tell my advisor was envious that my sister hadn't been her student, but I was completely unfazed and Chloe was none the wiser and highly unconcerned, beaming at me proudly.

Suddenly, I felt an unshakable sense of unease. I found myself maneuvering through the crowds of people. I felt like a child who'd gotten lost in a supermall, in a hurried search for their parents.

Except I didn't quite know what or who I was looking for. Had I excused myself before leaving the conversation? I didn't remember.

I stumbled into another professor with whom I'd been close, Iris, who was actually best friends with Frank. She embraced me in a hug, and while I normally let my arms dangle by my sides when people hug me, I felt, in that moment, the need to be held. I hugged back. After releasing each other, I grinned dumbly at her, my eyes welling up. I whipped around to hide my tears from Iris.

As I turned, I found my view blocked by a burly chest covered in a garish robe, inches from my face. I looked around, and hadn't noticed that all of the professors were wearing the same, gaudy robes. Why did I choose to ignore them up until now?

My eyes searched around frantically, feeling as though I had just been transported to a circus, with people laughing, crying, flashing camera lights illuminating people's grinning faces, making everyone look clownish, maniacal. I brought my head slowly forward, in line with the chest that had made me aware of the spectacle around me, following the robe lining to Frank's smiling face.

I found myself returning the sentiment, smirking back at him, and holding out a hand for him to shake. Head tilted in disapproval, Frank smacked my hand away and grabbed me, squeezing me a little too tightly. I hadn't really known what I was looking for, combing through the crowd, yet my face was buried in exactly what I wanted. I let myself rub my face into his chest, not knowing or caring who was looking at us.

This was one of those moments where it'd be okay for me to be a little more affectionate with anyone around me. I clutched onto him. I felt myself letting a smile spread across my face, and I let myself stay there longer than I should have, far too happy. I envisioned my teeth as a fence, protecting me from the outside world.

It wasn't nearly as bad as I'd thought it'd be. Nothing ever was.

"Cathy!"

Hearing the deafening sound of the nickname only reserved for family members, I knew the wall I'd let erect around me was soon to crumble. I allowed myself a few lingering moments to hide my face in Frank. Looking up, I caught a glimpse of a pretty blonde woman, sprinting toward me, followed closely by my step-father. My mother squealed with delight, always so proud of me for finishing anything.

I'd felt like I was being coddled, or that people walked on eggshells around me in a way that I never really required. Did everyone think I was capable of less? It was difficult for me to say why, and I chose not to ask because I'd decided it'd had nothing to do with me, but more of how people felt about me. Or was it me? Was there a reason why people were overly proud of me for normal things most people did?

My train of thought was interrupted by a blinding flash. I flinched instinctively and shut my eyes, pulling Frank toward myself to bury my face into his chest once more. Realization hitting me, I pushed myself away from him, glancing quickly and guiltily up at his face, and then toward the jarring flashes.

It had hit me that my parents had just happened upon me, my face pressed into Frank's chest, and then using his body again as comfort to protect myself from the offensive sparks from the camera. I'd hoped they hadn't picked up on the nature of the situation—seeing as I wasn't quite sure what I'd thought of it as well—and proceeded to stride over to my mother, grinning as much as I could stand before embracing her, then my stepfather. I'd imagined my affections, few and far between, might have prevented any further thoughts about my exchange with Frank.

I tended most times to be quite rigid around my parents, and so I figured any suspicions could be dissuaded by showing them something special, a treat. My parents felt as though my lack of warmth toward them was punishing, as opposed to understanding that was how I operated naturally. I felt bad, pitied that they felt as though all of my intentions were malicious, and so I threw them bones here and there, to which they fetched eagerly.

My mother, tears in her eyes, grabbed me after my stepfather released me, and held me at arm's length in front of her. Unequivocally, she was proud. I found myself, too, with my eyes welling up with tears, seeing her unashamed in her emotions. I'd always found it difficult to stifle tears when someone cried in front of me.

She pulled me in tightly, once more, and squeezed me until my ribs cracked and my stepfather placed a gentle hand on her shoulder, to usher her to allow others to have some of my attention. Quietly, she sobbed that she knew, and reluctantly released me. Wiping her face with her bare hands, leaning her head on my step dad's shoulder, she let out a whimper before composing herself with a question to detract attention from herself.

"So! Is this your professor?"

I did a double take and looked behind, seeing Frank standing where I'd left him, as he chatted with Chloe, who'd followed me over from the circus tent. He seemed to notice me whip around shocked, and made friendly eye contact and waved at my parents. Why was Frank still standing there? Weren't there other students to congratulate, other people to mingle with?

Part of me expected him to get lost after seeing my parents come toward me, like a boyfriend sneaking out of a window when his high school girlfriend's parents come home early from work.

This, naturally, had not been the case at all. And, as far as everyone knew—Chloe aside—he was simply what my mother asked: my professor.

Frank walked up to both of my parents to shake their hands, his long, wizard sleeves bouncing in sync with my stomach churning.

"Sure, so, he's an English professor here. I've only taken a few of his classes. He knows Chloe, too, actually."

I cast Chloe an apologetic look, thinking that I could somehow smear blame or guilt or fault by associating as many individuals with Frank as possible, but she didn't seem to mind and gave me a knowing smile.

Iris marched over as well to introduce herself to my parents, and my mom asked, "Could I get a picture of you three?"

Dumbfounded, I shot looks at Iris and Frank, both of them looking down at me proudly, and I thought it weirder to decline. I gave a small nod, seeing as I hated photos, no matter who they were with, and I began to give an uncomfortable smile before meeting the blinding flash once more.

"Another? Cathy, you blinked."

I let out a heavy sigh. I felt Frank's arm around my shoulder, and Iris followed suit, and I decided to stretch my arms behind their backs. I turned slightly toward Frank's chest, letting out a smile, bracing myself for the next flash.

Two Sets of Keys

I found myself at Frank's nearly every night the week after graduation, positively giddy and terrified to finally have completed university. Not only was I finished, but after making a few rounds at graduation, one of my favorite economics professors approached me to offer me a paid internship. I had been blindsided, seeing as I never felt as though I'd been the type to stand out from a crowd.

She assured me that she had been intrigued by my mathematics thesis speech and thought I'd be perfect for this research role. I accepted without hesitation and I found myself needing to stay in town for at least another three months to fulfill the contract. A weight was lifted off of me, knowing that I had something lined up for the summer, another long-term decision I could put off. For now.

I'd realized that I hadn't even told Frank that I intended on staying. Part of me felt like he didn't think I would be staying much longer anyway. Frank, himself, had quite a few things on his mind after graduation, and in a week, he'd be leaving for Seoul for a month on his annual trip to help students get their teaching certificates.

"So," Frank started, plopping down on his sectional next to me. "Have you figured out what you'd be doing for the summer?"

Finally, I'd had an answer to this question I had up until recently dreaded. I couldn't quite read his face, but he seemed a bit more reserved than usual, distant, even. I inched myself away from him before responding.

"Oh, yes, so I actually got offered a research internship. I'll be here til the end of summer,"

There was a pause.

Frank's face lit up and I felt my eyes widen in surprise, which may have made me look happier than I had meant to.

"CCC! You have no idea how happy that makes me!"

Me too, I thought, although for very different reasons. I no longer had to make any decisions, or respond in a manner that exhibited a balance of appearing unaffected without being lazy.

All while hiding the fact that I was, as a matter of fact, lazy and highly concerned.

"As you know," he repeated in a hyper tone, "I'm going to be really busy this summer..."

It always bothered me when people repeat themselves, or told the same story or joke multiple times. Did people not listen, or did people feel like no one was ever listening?

When telling a joke more than once, was it because it was such a hit the first time, or because they didn't remember telling it before?

How quickly can we actually pick up on those around us, especially when no one seems to be paying attention? No one listens, everyone just talks, and—

"CCC, do you have any nicknames?" Frank mused dreamily.

"Oh. Hm. You heard one of them, I suppose." I said cringing, thinking about my mom squealing "Cathy!" at graduation. Frank grinned.

"I thought it was cute, actually, but I mean, any other nicknames. Does anyone call you Cat?"

I took him through my general explanation, the same one I always tell everyone.

"Well, I generally just introduce myself as Catherine. My family calls me Cathy, my friends call me Cat, and a select group of people call me Birdy."

I'd realized that I, too, had a thing I'd repeated to most people. I became entirely self-conscious, knowing people had probably also rolled their eyes at how contrived that explanation was, especially upon hearing it more than once.

Fortunately, Frank had never heard my rehearsed introduction. It only further piqued his curiosity, and he pressed further.

"I want to call you something no one has ever called you, though."

"Well, technically, you have." I retorted.

Frank stared at me dumbly, and I laughed, saying "Beautiful."

After a few seconds, he remembered and let out a laugh before tilting his head downward, a faux-serious look spreading across his face.

"But, you didn't like that."

I didn't find myself particularly ugly, but I always hated attention called to my looks at all. This, to the extent that I've been cutting my own hair since I was 13, only making snips here and there, trimming the dead ends. To the untrained eye, the changes in my hair were forever undetectable. I'd hated when people would notice or comment on a haircut, or a drastic change in my physical appearance.

"How about Rin? Does anyone call you Rin?"

As a consequence, I'd actually gotten pretty decent at cutting hair, Chloe even entrusting me on occasion to give her a trim. Once, upon Chloe's request, my grandmother took her to a family friend's hair salon for a haircut. Aunty Flo, as we knew her, studied and observed Chloe's ends, and inquired as to who had most recently cut her hair.

"Cathy," Chloe stated, staring at herself in the mirror, unperturbed.

"Okay, so if not beautiful, then unbeautiful?"

Aunty Flo, gingerly holding Chloe's hair in both her hands, letting the strands slip through her fingers like trickles of water, looked into the mirror's reflection at me, seated almost directly behind Chloe, and then her gaze darted toward our grandmother. Aunty Flo's head, jerking toward me without taking her eyes off of my grandmother, said I did a damn good job. My grandmother considered me for an instant and reading my vacant face gave a slight smile.

"Well," Aunty Flo continued, "Anyway, I'm sure she doesn't get along with the world."

My grandmother laughed and nodded generously.

I hadn't been able to determine the inflections of Frank's questions, confusing Frank's questions with the conversation I was playing out in my head. I couldn't remember where I was supposed to be, and with whom. Was I on the couch, with a man? Or was I in a hair salon, staring at my own reflection while people talked about me as if I wasn't there? It was hard for me to determine which felt more real.

The strangeness of these words helped me determine which scenario was more accurate. I tested a response.

"If it has to be between beautiful, or unbeautiful, I suppose I prefer the latter. However, no one has called me Rin before. I rather like it."

The words escaped my mouth, and as they left, I was able to find my grip on the couch.

I was on a couch, in a living room.

My approval of a unique nickname seemed to trump the fact that I had actively parted ways with our conversation without so much of an explanation.

"Okay, Rin. I'll call you Rin, or CCC, or unbeautiful."

He was radiating warmth, and happiness, and I absorbed some of his light. I had never seen anyone so truly happy to see me, someone who couldn't stop looking at me in the way that he did. It seemed impossible for me not to be drawn to him, be in his company, to be important to him. Sadness overcame me, as the thought of him being away for a month as of next week reoccurred to me.

Funny enough, I had forgotten, if only for a moment, that he was leaving, despite him having told me multiple times. A sharp pang hit me in the chest, and I nuzzled up next to him. Frank excused himself for a moment, to which I had assumed was the restroom. I heard some wooden drawers open and close, and he returned immediately with something shiny pinched between his fingers: a set of keys.

"Here, I'll be gone for a month, so I want you to be able to come through, whenever you want, and feel like this is your home, too. It'd be comforting for me to know that you're here, reading, living, enjoying, inhabiting. Really, and you can always keep it."

He dropped the keys into my hands that seemed to have suddenly been extended without me noticing, and I brought them up to my eyes, observing them. I tried to find a flaw in the key, a warning asserting that the keys should not be duplicated, or a curious nick, or anything for me to make a joke about, but there was nothing. They were new, glimmering, catching light at every angle. I couldn't take my eyes off of them.

"Do you know why I want you to have these?" Frank whispered.

I thought about how exciting it would be to have a spare set of keys, two sets on me at all times, and how I'd get to be careful while searching in my purse to ensure that I was grabbing the correct pair to enter my car, a small trophy I'd collected, earned.

There was always something so invigorating about having a secret under people's noses.

"Rin, it's because I love you."

I dropped the keys.

"What did you say?"

Frank paused, smiling, strong in his convictions.

"I love you and I want us to be together."

I looked down at the ground, and then picked up the keys from my lap. I stared at the secret trophy in my hands. I tightened my grip, but only so I could no longer look at it.

"No, Frank, you don't."

16 Hours Ahead

The next morning, despite my offer to drive him, Frank took a shuttle he'd booked to the airport, saying that it'd been too last minute to cancel what he'd already reserved. We'd decided that I'd be available to pick him up in a months' time, after returning from Seoul.

Frank left early, kissing me on my cheek as I stirred. In my sleepy stupor, I wished him a safe flight. In and out of sleep, I only heard some of what he'd been saying to me as he was leaving, as I let out gentle grunts and sighs of affirmation, to show that I understood and that I was listening, even though it was only partially the case.

"..and I'll miss you,"

"mhm..."

"and I love you..."

"hm."

"and no rush, but don't forget to lock up when you leave."

"mmm."

Through one half opened eye, I saw Frank fussing about the room, occasionally stealing quick, frantic glances at me. I couldn't tell why my presence had seemed to make him suddenly so uncomfortable. I chose not to awaken, so as not to have to listen to any further instructions or to accept more responsibility than I'd wanted.

Grabbing his suitcases, he peered down at me, and said he was off. I let my eyes flutter open for a second, and smiled lightly as I wished him a safe flight. Frank's eyes glistened slightly seeing mine grace his, but something in them still felt sad, unfulfilled. He left and closed the door softly, his head hung down.

I let myself drift in and out of sleep for a few more hours. Rejoining the waking world reluctantly, I propped myself up, rubbing my eyes, staring into the dark bedroom. It felt strange, being in a place that I'd only ever been in with another person, one specific person, alone. My eyes swept the room, still hooded in darkness from his curtains. I felt an eerie loss that I couldn't comprehend.

I let my arms slip out from under me to allow my body to flop back on the bed. Staring up at the ceiling, I started to come to terms with the fact that I'd be Frankless for an entire month. Was that a bad thing? Every time I was with him, I couldn't help but find flaws, to nitpick everything that bothered me, to essentially tear him apart as he stood before me, beaming at me with nothing but the kindest affections.

Yet, now, here I was without him, and I felt as though something was taken from me. There was an empty space in the bed, nothing to hold his place. I closed my eyes, suppressing the loss, and decided to dissect what had happened before he left. Frank kept looking over at me, almost frightened, as though I'd wounded him and he was waiting again for me to attack.

Had I said something? I didn't think I had. I'd been too tired to have been able to formulate full sentences or words, and couldn't have imagined I'd actually said anything offensive. I tried to recall the things he'd said to me. He'd miss me... well, I'd certainly already felt him gone. Cold, empty. I suppose I did miss him.

I hadn't said it back to him, and perhaps he'd assumed that I would? Did I even know that I would miss him when he left? And if I did, did I know the feeling would hit me this quickly? Mere hours after he left, in the same place in which he left me, how was it possible to miss someone this viscerally?

Okay, so, I missed him.

Perhaps he was unaware of that, but it was true. And I'd tell him when I got the chance. That box sorted and checked in my mind, I fought to sift through the haze of my dreaminess, and remembered suddenly that he'd said he loved me. He said it this morning, yes, but he'd also said it last night. Naturally, I hadn't said it back, but to be fair, I almost never said it back. Not at first, anyway.

When I was young, I had this romanticized idea of saying "I love you". It had to be well into the relationship, that it had to be a sudden moment or building of moments that reached a crescendo of overwhelming emotion, longing, everything for a person. The boys and men I'd dated had always said it too fast, as though they were in some rush to get more out of the situation, either for sex, or because their friends had all said the phrase to their girlfriends and they felt left behind.

I'd dated someone quite a bit older than me when I was a freshman in high school, who told me he loved me after only two weeks of our relationship being official. He'd made quite a grand gesture of it, acting very dramatic and saying there was something important he'd needed to discuss with me. I'd even gone out of my way to visit him on his lunch break at work, in which he spent the majority of the half hour panicky and ruffled. Finally, he said, "it's only been two weeks, and I fucking love you." He kissed me, stood up abruptly, and walked back into work.

I'd known, deep down, that he'd only said it to expedite the timeline of us having sex. Had he known, though, that I was planning on sleeping with him very soon regardless, I do feel as though he would have said I love you, anyway. Not only was he one for theatrics, but a week after we'd finally slept together, he'd gotten a tattoo for me.

Perhaps "for me" isn't the best way to describe it. I'd begged him not to when he'd told me he'd been toying with the idea.

A few months later, he'd cheated on me with his ex-girlfriend.

My college boyfriend also dropped "I love you" out of nowhere, less than a few weeks after we'd been dating, to which I spat back viciously, "No, you don't."

I couldn't take the empty words. I'd always felt so disappointed in how my thoughts of the phrase, the words, the feeling never really seemed to match up to what I'd wanted or what I thought it meant.

This boyfriend in particular, got sulky that I hadn't said it back, and it dawned on me that my thoughts about love, the expectations and the word I'd put on a pedestal had a different meaning to everyone. Because of its purely subjective and ever-changing meaning to people across individual understandings, and within relationships, the word itself untrue and unstable, a word I could not control, this word love no longer meant anything to me.

It was then, I walked over to this sweet 18-year-old boy, as a hardened, jaded 18-year-old girl, knelt down to where he'd sunken on his dorm room desk chair, grabbed his face, kissed him, and said "I love you, too."

So then, was it settled? I hadn't said "I love you" to Frank, but did I need to feel it to say it?

What was that feeling, anyway? I wasn't sure I'd even know what to look for, what to feel. Wasn't it just something to say? Like, if someone cooks food for you, and asks how it is, don't you just say it's great regardless of whether or not it's true? Or if someone introduces you to a new boyfriend or girlfriend, and then asks what you think of them, don't you say they're nice even if they're completely awful? Saying you love someone, it's just a kindness, a pleasantry. Pretty, empty words.

Rejuvenated, I shot up out of bed. Sure, I could say all those things easily, without hesitation from this point forward, to appease the instigator. What was it to me, but a "you too" or a "sounds good". It was certainly better than a hurt look, someone afraid to come near me as though my silence was a viper strike against them. Yes, yes. Next time, in person. I would say it back.

Okay, so. He missed me. He loved me. I thought again to the words I could recollect, and remembered: the keys. I looked at the nightstand at the keys he'd left for me. He wanted me to lock up, to take care of his place. There was no security system or anything of the like, because he'd thought putting out the ADT security system flag in his front yard without actually having the security set up would be enough to thwart potential robbers. Clever, I thought, but I was also grateful I didn't have to fiddle with a security system.

Gathering my belongings, I made my way downstairs. At the foot of the stairs were my shoes, by the door, and as I began to slip them on, I noticed a piece of paper, balanced precariously on the laces.

"CCC, I miss you again, already, still…"

My heart fluttered, and read the note over a few times, admiring his penmanship, the fact that the pen was felt, not the type of pen anyone would normally carry around with them. A pen tip that was rarely meant for anything in particular, aside from, perhaps, notes like this.

I drove home in a daze, and arrived in the late afternoon.

My apartment was dark, empty, and I wasn't sure which place would make me feel more alone. My own apartment, I was used to being alone in. People, things, places to be were all outside but I could retreat here when it was all too much. Now, it felt as though everything that was too much was within me, following me, sucking the life out of any room or space I occupied.

I sat on the couch, staring at the blank TV. I knew I shouldn't be inside, by myself, and decided to reach out to Chase to see if he'd had any plans, so I could give myself an outing to look forward to. Attempting to distract myself by any and all means necessary, I snatched my laptop and began preparing for my internship that would be starting the first of the following month.

Scanning through my emails, I found a new one with the subject line "hey, unbeautiful". I laughed out of relief, as though I had forgotten to breathe, and clicked open the email from Frank.

"You know what I'm going to do? I'm going to read myself to sleep and sleep earlier than I have in a long time… so, there! Still, I really wish you were here (or me there) to play.

But instead of that, I'm going to read and enjoy it. Haven't read enough of late.

-Me"

I hadn't lost the chance to tell him what I needed to say. Now, I could say I wished he was here too, or vice versa. I'd have to think of something witty to hide my discomfort, my feelings. This weird sense of nothingness I'd suddenly felt. I didn't want Frank to know that, of course.

In the subject line, I wrote "next week is my" and continued the rest of the sentence in the body of the email. "birthday. I'm going to force some friends to accompany me to Portland to celebrate. Care to join?"

We'd regularly joke about inviting each other to things we knew the other couldn't possibly join.

"I wish you were here, and there, and back."

I wrote that, just that, and I sent it.

I think, too, that I meant it.

Birthdays Abound

After catching up with Chase, we'd decided to take a short road trip down to Portland to celebrate both of our birthdays. As luck would have it, Chase's birthday was less than a week after mine, which helped me to find a half-excuse to get out of the house and celebrate. I'd never been one to really enjoy my birthdays because the idea of aging, responsibilities, decisions, always scared me.

The notion that age equated to experience, and that experience led to needing to make better choices. I didn't feel capable of making better choices. Being older, to me, meant being better, being correct, and I wasn't quite sure how to achieve that idea. I never felt ready for it.

Chloe had cared to join Chase and I, and she brought along a guy she'd only recently started seeing named Russell. The four of us decided to drive to Portland together, and share a hotel room. Russell was in charge of driving, because he enjoyed it, he said, but also perhaps to get on Chloe's good side, showing a kindness to her younger sister and friend.

Chase and I excitedly discussed the hell we were about to raise for our birthdays, deciding that we'd do a strip club tour of Portland, and get super drunk at some of his favorite bars. Naturally, his girlfriend Beth wouldn't be joining us, even though we'd told her she'd be more than welcome to.

Chase's demeanor suddenly darkened as he leaned his head toward me in the backseat.

"You can't tell Beth we're sharing a bed."

I didn't even waste my time laughing, because I knew he was already wildly ashamed to warn me, covering his tail.

"You have nothing to worry about. We'll never meet, so nothing will ever slip out."

Chase, wounded, pulled back a bit, and in an effort to smooth the conversation over, I suggested that he share a bed with Russell, if that would be a better arrangement for him. Chase scoffed, shaking his head, and turned forward.

"Don't be weird…"

We arrived at the hotel, and the four of us began jumping up and down childishly on the beds, hopping back and forth, discussing between panting and catching our breaths, and we'd decided to start off the day doing fun, touristy things before we eventually ventured off in our separate ways. Russell and Chloe didn't drink at all, and seemed to have no interest in our more questionable plans for the evening.

As Chloe and Russell headed back to the hotel room, Chase and I were free to unleash ourselves. Bar hopping, we discussed what types of strip clubs we'd eventually find.

"The strip clubs in Portland are the best. Truly. They're large, lavish, the women are hot and they're fun and attentive. You'll absolutely love it."

Chase recounted detailed excursions he'd been on previously, regaling me with his run ins, his friends and he astronomically drunk, and doing essentially what we'd hoped to do in Portland ourselves. Chase and I sat alongside each other, making an actual list on the back of a receipt with all of the strip clubs we'd intended to go to, hopefully with pit stops at the dingiest, shittiest looking bars on the way. Pulling up our phones to map our trek, we decided the best course of action, gulped down the remaining liquid in our glasses, and ventured off.

The first bar was a tavern that had saloon-type swinging doors. I burst through them animatedly, all while accidently smacking a few of the patrons nearest to the doors. I glanced at them, put my head down with a smidgen of remorse and apologized in a barely genuine manner, which seemed to be enough for the battered customers, who turned around immediately and resumed their conversations.

Chase and I moved around the crowds to get to the bar, and retrieving our drinks, we sunk down into our bar stools, decorated with stirrups. I looked at the adorned walls, rife with whips, spurs, old photos of cowboys on their horses.

One photo that hung above us was a handsome cowboy on his horse, the look on his face suggestive, as though the photographer were a naked woman. I imagined her summoning him over with that worming, inching finger gesture that only kind of makes sense to me.

I stared at the horse, which had a glazed, lifeless expression. I thought about what happened after the picture was taken, and if the photographer nonchalantly dropped the camera, and jumped on the horse to mount the cowboy. I imagined that, had they started passionately having sex on top of the horse, the horse would have stayed statuesquely still, unfazed by the movement and tugging and grunting on top of him.

That is, of course, if they were able to maintain their balance on top of the horse. If they happened to roll off—which I'm sure they would have—they'd land on the horse shit-laden grass, rolling around, while the horse stared off into the distance, with the intent and direction of someone who'd just had a lobotomy.

"So! Where's mister PhD? He didn't want to join us for your birthday festivities?"

My eyes following the photo to the bottom of the frame, dropped back down to Chase, meeting his eyes.

"Oh, he's in Seoul."

Chase scoffed playfully, and putting his beer down he mused, "man. What a cool life he has. You didn't want to go with him?"

Did I want to? I wasn't sure I'd want to join Frank on this trip if it meant returning back to the same power dynamic we'd had before. Sure, I'd graduated, but he would have to essentially take care of me, and I'd also need to actually be interested in the teaching course he'd be a part of. Our relationship was still very much under wraps. I hadn't told anyone outside of immediate friends, and my sister. I couldn't imagine letting anyone else know outside of whom I'd already told. What would people say? Did I care? Was it something I'd needed to preface before introducing him to anyone new?

"Hello, this is my..."

Wait. I'd forgotten that we hadn't really even made anything official. I heaved in a sort relieved manner, and looked at Chase, who'd been watching me with a look of semi-concern. His brows were furrowed and his eyes narrowed, as though he was genuinely worried about my well-being, but his mouth was curled into a clown-like smile as he watched the gears turning in my head.

"Ready to join the outside world?"

I'd decided to tell Chase what Frank had said, about loving me.

"Well, that was fast. What'd you do to the poor guy?"

I laughed. "The older you get, the less time you have. He must be in a rush or something."

Chase giggled at my willingness to play along with his old-jokes, and then turned the question to me.

"Well?"

I knew what he was asking, but I wasn't sure what to tell Chase. I decided to play dumb on the off chance Chase would drop the subject.

"Well, what?"

"Don't give me that shit. What did you say to him? Did you say it back? Do you love him? Do you think he actually loves you?"

I hadn't considered that he hadn't loved me outside of the context of what I used to think love was before. Did he really love me? What would he be wanting to get out of me by saying that? We were already having sex—if that's what you could call it—and. Well, what else was there? Commitment? I suppose we'd yet to have that discussion, and I wasn't sure what I'd say, or what I'd really even wanted.

"I didn't say it back. It sort of came out of nowhere, so I was a bit taken aback."

"Well, do you think so?"

It was times like this that made me despise Chase for how attentive and deep he was. He'd know that there was a difference between what people say and don't say, and what they feel and don't feel. What should I tell Chase? Should I be honest and say, maybe I did, in the context of this relationship, think I love Frank?

Would it be cooler to be confident and stronger in my convictions? Or should I go on with my attitude, shrugging him off and continuing to use Frank as the butt of all of our jokes for the rest of the evening? Was there anything in the middle?

I'd suddenly realized what I imagine goes through Chase's head when he's making the decisions to appease his male co-workers, or respect his girlfriend's wishes. It felt weird to play two sides of a coin, and honestly, it did just feel easier to lie to save face to anyone around you. I took a few large sips of beer.

"Honestly, I'm. Yeah, maybe I do love him."

Chase's mouth gaped open wide in shock, and he laughed fully and loudly in my face.

"Aw. Catherine! That's..." he stopped mid-sentence and continued to stare at my face, which I'd then begun to be aware of.

"You're. Huh. You're serious, right? You mean it?"

I looked down at the beer in my hands, and gave it a little swirl.

"I mean, I don't really know what love is, but I feel like it's turning into something more than what I'd initially thought it'd be."

This was a partially true statement, because with most of my actions, I don't think about the repercussions. As with most of my decisions, I didn't really consider what I had wanted out of the situation before accepting his invitation to the strip club.

Or before agreeing to go to his house after that.

Or sleeping with him. Or continuing to sleep with him.

Chase, at a loss, looked down at his beer and peered up at the lobotomy cow.

"Well, I can honestly say I'm surprised, but I'm happy for you. Can I meet him at some point? It'd be cool to get to know the guy."

Grateful for Chase's approval, I nodded and smiled in acquiescence.

Hours passed, and somehow in a flurry of alcohol and people, Chase and I neglected to enter a single strip club, getting completely shit housed drunk to the point of barely being able to stand up straight. Resigned to our failed plan, we laughed and held each other up on the sidewalk as we hailed a taxi to take us back to the hotel.

Drunk, friendly, and rambling, I was talking the taxi driver's ear off about strip clubs and asking him if he had any recommendations. The driver obligingly discussed which ones were most popular, careful not to say that he enjoyed going there, but the ones he'd noticed his passengers or others wanting to attend.

"Which one is your favorite?"

"Oh no, miss. I don't do that kind of stuff."

"Huh. Fine."

Drunk out of my mind, I hadn't noticed until we were almost at the hotel that Chase had been abnormally silent. Turning to look at him, his eyes closed, he was huddled against the door, looking as though he were suffering through a cold and vicious winter. As we pulled up to the curb, I touched Chase's arm to wake him up, and turned back to the taxi driver to give him some cash for the ride. The driver's eyes on my hand found their way to Chase. He pointed slowly at Chase, who had flung the door wide open and was on all fours, vomiting profusely outside of the vehicle. I apologized and thanked the driver, handed him the money, and walked around the other side of the car to help Chase up off the pavement. After a long, limping walk, we finally made it to the room, and I let him slump onto the bed, where he immediately curled up in a miserable looking ball and passed out.

Unready to commit to bed, I tiptoed to the bathroom and sat on the floor. I didn't want to wake anyone else up by turning on any lights in the main room. I sat on the cold linoleum, squinting at the brightness around me. I sighed, and leaned my head against the wall with my eyes closed. I normally do a personal-belongings safety check before leaving a bar, and it occurred to me I hadn't done one all night. I scrambled for my bag, and found the essentials: phone, wallet, keys.

I heaved a sigh of relief, and placed everything back into my bag, still holding on to my phone. I opened my emails, craving to find something from Frank. I'd found myself feeling open, vulnerable, because of what I had told Chase, and although it had not been to Frank, I wanted some kind of validation from him, a sign that I hadn't admitted that to my friend for no reason. I wanted proof or evidence that I had made the right decision to say I love him.

My eyes feasted upon the subject line "Happy".

Greedily, I clicked open the email.

"Birthday, Rin. One year older, wiser, more beautiful… ahem, I mean, unbeautiful. This made me think of you. I miss you."

The attached photo had been of a woman, hacking at a dozen dead frogs, blood spattering the metal sink and counter, her butcher knife suspended mid-chop.

Now was my chance, I could say I missed him as well. One wrong righted. I stared at the picture, and studied the gutted frogs in awe. The blood was pure red, honest. I saw a pink, seedless strawberry next to each of the frogs, and noticed that they were each of the little frogs' hearts. I couldn't take my eyes off the photo, seeing the blood drops from the knife, the look of bored on the woman's face. I'd wished I could see any of the frogs' eyes in the photo, wondering if they'd have the same type of horse-glazed look, or if they'd be wide with fear. Had they died by her hand, or were they killed humanely before?

After a minute, my phone screen turned black from inactivity, and I caught a glimpse of my own reflection, my eyes wide in twisted fascination.

Murderous, ravenous.

The face of a woman in love.

A College Party

A few weeks had passed, and Frank's Wi-Fi connections proved more and more unreliable, the emails and photos in which I craved became fewer and further between. As much as I understood that he'd missed me and wanted to contact me, I couldn't deny that I'd felt pathetic, turning on my email notifications and checking my phone compulsively.

Chase and Chloe kept asking me for updates and checking in on me, but I would resort to brushing them off. Never wanting to admit feelings that made me look what I considered lesser than, I kept this feeling of emptiness close to my chest.

My internship was incredibly monotonous and boring, and I knew that none of my research and spreadsheets were actually going to be utilized. The contact at the county actually hadn't even bothered to pay me yet and was avoiding all emails that concerned forms of payment. I looked around the apartment, grateful to have saved from my previous part time jobs and stacked enough of my student loans to pay for the last couple of months on the lease.

Every daily activity, punctuated by a phone call or an impromptu social outing with Chase, felt like I was just going through the motions. The feelings of longing only semi-satiated by a photo, an email, anything. There was an end in sight, and these little bursts of communication kept me going.

I'd been most excited initially about our most recent exchange, in which the subject line read "The back of the library." Opening the attachment, there was the back of a drab, lifeless building, amorphous without signage. It was funny, truly, including a caption stating "isn't it lovely?".

But I was disappointed. These were the types of emails we'd exchanged before anything happened between us. As much as I told myself I would take what I could get, receiving emails like this now, when his emails were rare treats, did nothing to satisfy me.

"What are you, on a smoke break? Usually only smokers subject themselves to such dreary views. Albeit, for no longer than ten minutes or so at a time."

Before sending, I read over my two lines, thinking that it was perfectly adequate for a text message, or something that'd garner immediate replies, but not one that would satisfy me for an extended period of time.

However, I had to remember he was not me. Was this all he needed? A quick touch base before he got to return to his world of excitement and wonder, while I had to continue to live my vacant reality, void of direction and meaning.

How did everything suddenly become about Frank? Was it just because my summer had been so slow, so unstimulating without him? My life, my identity, before him revolved around school, and now that it was over, I had free time, and nothing to do with it.

My phone buzzed, indicating a text message—although my heart did flutter—and I opened a message from my friend inviting me to a party. He was a foreign exchange student who would be heading back home and was hosting his own farewell party. I replied at an embarrassingly fast rate, and felt another wave of temporary relief.

I had plans tonight, something to say I was doing. I was never known as someone who'd attended many parties during university, but tended to stick within a small group of friends. I felt an unnecessary amount of gratitude to have plans for the evening, because saying no to invites usually leads to fewer of them, and I needed this now more than ever.

There was something lonely, sad about never being invited to anything, especially when I had nothing to occupy my time. But now, I had this party. I could drink, and make friends, and I thought I'd have enough to say, even though that wasn't the case. I could say "paid internship with the county" because it was true on paper, and people wouldn't think to ask what I'd been doing with my free time. They'd assume I'd be going into a secure-access building, busy, important. In actuality, I was filling out spreadsheets from the comfort of my couch, communicating with the faculty advisor via email.

What else could I say, though? Who had I seen and what else had I done? Did I actually have anything planned? No current vacations, nothing tentative. I guess I could tell everyone I was thinking about moving back home. At the end of the day, you only really had to answer people's questions to a certain extent, right?

Conversations were just reaching a quota, so I just had to find the sweet spot between saying enough to not sound like I was hiding something or being evasive, because then that would invite more probing. I didn't want to overshare... what if I got too drunk and I'd let it slip in a room full of current and previous students that knew Frank that I'd been fucking him?

This must have been the stress adults feel when they don't see their peers for a while. There's no pressure to have something interesting to say when people see you walking around campus every day, when they know your major and your extracurricular activities, and every day has very little noticeable difference.

Was this how my conversations for the rest of my life would be? Not seeing my old friends, and acquaintances for a long enough period of time where I'd have to relay my life updates, over exaggerating at each and every party invitation I'd begrudgingly accept.

I imagined every family household I'd been to, walls adorned with holiday cards and letters. Paragraphs and paragraphs about what everyone had been up to, as if anyone cared. Why did people write those cards? Is it so that people wouldn't ask questions? Or was it more of the opposite: conversations would be easier, talking points provided?

Okay, so internship, maybe moving, and how else was I utilizing my time? I suppose the rest of my days would be filled with other things, like my hobbies. What were my hobbies? It was daunting to repeat to every person who approached me at a party about my interests. I enjoyed reading, writing, and even though I was technically doing both of those things through my internship, I hadn't actually been reading or writing things I'd wanted to read or write about.

I decided to tell everyone I was running, because exercise seemed to be an activity that didn't require much proof or output aside from physical changes. What other type of exercise could I say I'd been doing? I couldn't afford a gym membership because I wasn't currently getting any of the income I'd been promised from the internship.

I decided to be a runner who also did yoga from watching videos online, since they were both free and required no equipment. Deciding on my identity for the party, a recent graduate with a paid internship who spends the rest of her time running and doing yoga and not fucking her professor, I was ready to socialize.

Arriving at the apartment on time for the gathering, I was greeted only by the hosts, who were shocked to see me there on time. I put my pack of beer in the fridge, grabbed one for myself, and snagged a stool to sit at near the counter. My friends, laying out the spread, slowly wiping down dusty surfaces made small talk with me.

"So," they started, "what have you been up to?"

I was ready.

The guests finally began to trickle in, and I was relieved to see many new faces. New people wouldn't ask questions too pressing, and the conversations could be kept superficial.

The party had about 20 people in total, with people staying only for an hour, showing face, before saying their goodbyes. Clutching onto my beer, I wasn't sure how to initiate conversation. Should I be trying to make new friends? Meeting the people I didn't know yet? Or should I stick with those whom I was already familiar with? I started drinking my beer much faster than I'd wanted to, calculating how long I'd want to stay at the party and how long I'd need my beer to last me, hiding in my corner.

I'd made a mental note of the apartment layout. Two bedrooms, two bathrooms, one of which was inside the master bedroom. A kitchen, open, attached to the living room. A balcony.

My friends began to sense the permanent partygoers, and suggested we play a drinking game. Sitting in a circle, my friend walked around and handed each of us a card. He explained that there was one king card and the rest were numbered. The cards are dealt out randomly, and whoever gets the king card gets to make a rule.

My friend handed me a card, which I lifted slightly toward my face and saw a 2 of hearts. This round's king was a guest I'd never met before, but he raised his card like a trophy.

"Even numbers! Remove an article of clothing!"

I looked around at half of the groaning room, and looked down at my clothes. Okay, luckily I hadn't worn a dress. I had regretted taking my socks off and putting them in my shoes when I'd entered, because surely I could have gotten away with counting each of them as two articles.

The other evens clearly had the same idea, as they gingerly began picking off their socks and placing them carefully next to themselves. I sighed audibly and removed my shirt.

Next round dealt, I peeled the card to my face to see a 7 of spades. My face fell, knowing that the evens had been targeted last time, so the odds would probably be next. My friend, the dealer, happened to be king.

"Hmm... 7 and 8. Kiss."

Stunned, I scanned each person in the circle across from me. I searched for someone's face who looked just as pale as mine had been.

"Uh. I'm 8."

I turned to my right and saw my friend Greg who had also just graduated sitting next to me. I looked straight ahead and flipped my card so that it would face him, laughing. We both threw our hands up in a motion suggesting resignation, and we began kissing.

His lips were soft, and his tongue was gentle, flowing. It felt comforting sharing that moment with him, and I even started lifting my hand up to his face, and ran my fingers through his soft hair. He moved his hand opposite mine to my face, brushing my hair behind my ear. He let his fingers fall, grazing my neck and I trembled before remembering people were watching.

I pulled myself away slowly, and looked at my friend, before looking down at the ground. I turned to face the group, and everyone began laughing and applauding. I jokingly went along with it, and pretended to bow and curtsy while still seated, stealing a glance from my friend who I'd just kissed. He pushed his glasses up to his face and grabbed his beer, drinking heavily from the bottle.

Next, 4 of diamonds. I stared at the card, wondering when people would call on the different suits. Evens, odds, those were easy to call out, by why not yell for the diamonds to—

"Diamonds! Remove an article of clothing!"

I chastised myself for being too critical, and stood up to remove my pants. I looked around the room at everyone still seated.

"I can't be the only diamond…"

Everyone showed their cards, and as it were, I could be the only diamond. I was the only diamond. I removed my pants, thankful that I hadn't worn anything skin-tight that would have been mortifying to struggle with, suggesting to everyone I was indeed lying about running and yoga this summer. I folded the pants and placed them on top of my shirt.

Sitting back down, I couldn't meet anyone's eye and accepted my new card bringing it down to meet my gaze. 9 of clubs.

"Odds, remove an article of clothing!"

I let out a wail and laughed in defeat, as my dealer friend stopped the current king.

"Okay, I think Catherine has had enough here. Choose something different."

"Fine. 9 and 4, kiss."

My head, already hung low, sunk even further into my hands. I started cackling, and everyone glared at me, laughing as well. I looked up at my friend who was about to protest once more and stopped him.

"It's okay. Clearly, it's meant to be."

I looked around at everyone once more, looking for four, and I heard a throat clear to the right of me. Greg was roped in with me again this round. I giggled, and we leaned in once more, people cheering for us before we even got started.

This time, we kissed a little more passionately, any hesitation we'd had the first time had gone out the window. Both of his hands framing my face, his lips parting and breathing into my mouth. Uncrossing my legs, I inched myself closer to him, feeling one of his hands move from my face, him turning his hands so his fingernails could graze my skin, cascading shivers over my body. I felt him smile and let out a soft laugh as he felt me quiver, and he let his hand end its journey resting on my thigh. Every fiber of my being wanted to keep going, to take it further.

"Uh, oh my god!"

We snapped back to reality, and I noticed people were shifting uncomfortably, some even had gotten up to use the bathroom and grab some drinks. I moved myself further away from my friend, and giggled again. I decided to lighten the tension.

"See? That's what happens when I'm constantly getting put through the ringer. Please, stop picking my number!"

Laughing, everyone settled back down and we decided to play one more round, winding down the evening. The next round required everyone to drink, starting with 2 and ending with 9, the fair king deciding to punish everyone instead of unintentionally targeting me.

Gasping for air jokingly after putting down my beer I had pretended to chug, I slowly began to dress myself and asked to use the restroom.

Staring at myself in the mirror, I noticed my lips looked plump, the most recent usage having caused an almost swollen reaction. I moved my face closer to my reflection, noticing how full of life they looked. Swelling with desire, I bit my lip and watched the bitten area turn white, before flooding back with color. I stood there for a minute, watching my teeth turn my bottom lip pale, the color ebbing and flowing in and out of my lips. I began to touch my lips with my fingertips, creating small white circles on them until I heard music blasting from the party in the living room.

Did I want to go back out there? I couldn't remember exactly where I'd left my purse, so I couldn't necessarily just leave without saying goodbye to anyone. Would anyone say anything to me anyway? Would anyone want to? They'd seen a whole lot of me this evening, and I'd hasten to assume any conversation would almost lead directly to what just happened. I thought about going home, and remembered how much I needed to get out, how much I wanted tonight. I was staying, like it or not. I had two more beers left, and I'd stay for as long as I needed to be okay to drive. I walked out of the bathroom, and waiting outside was Greg.

"Oh, hey..." he said, pushing his glasses up again. "I was just going to use the bathroom..."

I moved out of the way for him, noticing my purse in the open coat closet across the bathroom. I grabbed my bag, and looked toward the door. It was right there, it was so easy to just leave. Did I need those two beers? Certainly, someone else would enjoy them. I picked up my phone, and checked my texts.

I was shocked to see someone I'd hooked up with throughout the school year texting me out of the blue. The quintessential "hey, you up?" type of message, although almost a weekly alert for me to take my place in his bed, had been nonexistent over the last couple of months.

I'd almost forgotten about him.

"Hey, long time no see. Actually, I've been drinking tonight, so I shouldn't drive anywhere. Rain check?"

"Sure. I respect that. Have fun and stay safe."

What I'd typed was right, though. I had been drinking, and I shouldn't leave the party yet. My friends had offered everyone to stay the night if they couldn't drive, so I decided to do the very un-me thing, and stay at the party. I placed my phone back in my bag, and shoved it back into the coat closet.

Rejoining everyone at the party, no one seemed at all put off or perturbed by me. I was half avoiding Greg and didn't want to stand next to him because I'd remembered another "long time no see" question that people ask: are you dating anyone? I couldn't—or I didn't—hide my obvious attraction to Greg, and how much I'd actually enjoyed kissing him. People would ask why we weren't dating and I didn't want to have that discussion. I decided, instead, to claim a blanket in an empty room and go to sleep.

Waking up around 6 am the next day with a sizable headache, I quietly untucked myself from the blanket and tiptoed toward the closet to find my bag to leave. I scanned the room and noticed a few others had spent the night as well, Greg included.

His eyes began to flutter open, and I tried to leave before he could see me. I made my way to the hallway, before hearing a groggy voice.

"Catherine? Wait. Can I talk to you?"

My heart sunk, and I walked back toward the room, watching Greg wobble upright, still wrapped in his blanket. He motioned that we talk in the living room, where no one else was, and we awkwardly walked out with each other.

"Catherine, how did you feel about that? About last night. Us kissing." He rushed the last sentence in, knowing that I'd try to weasel my way out of responding directly to his questions.

"Well, I mean. It was good. Weird? I don't really know."

"The truth is, I've wanted to do that for a long time now."

My heart stopped. I'd had no idea that Greg had any remote attraction for me, let alone that kissing me was something he'd been wanting to do for a while now. I thought about how good last night felt, how badly I wanted him, how if no one else was watching, how far would I be able to actually go? It was weird to think about him like that, because I'd never considered it before.

Fuck. Frank.

He had completely slipped my mind the entire night. Had I done what I did last night out of spite? Had I been jealous, and felt abandoned? Is that why I thought kissing Greg was so amazing? Did I miss Frank's touch? Or was Greg's touch what I actually wanted?

I took a step back from Greg still wrapped in his blanket, his eyes falling to the floor, looking a bit like a child who had been reprimanded by a parent. I walked up to Greg, and put my cheek up to his. I felt him tremble, his cheek getting warmer as I breathed into his ear.

I slowly moved my mouth closer to his, hesitating for a moment, allowing him to move his lips up toward mine to kiss me again. It was soft, softer than the first time we'd kissed. I dropped my bag on the ground, heat rising from my chest, and we stood there, kissing, alone in the living room.

Greg dropped his blanket, and grabbed me, pinning me up to the wall, kissing me more ferociously, more and more eager with each and every breath. I felt him harden against my stomach, and I scrambled to get his belt unbuckled. Greg played with the bottom end of my shirt, hinting that he'd wanted it off if I was okay with it, and as I started to lift it up myself, he slid his hands underneath, massaging my breasts. I let out an unexpected high-pitch moan, and frantically tried to get his belt off of him.

I felt his fingers make their way under my bra, and he toyed with my nipples. I felt myself melt into him, wanting so badly to feel him inside of me.

Right then, a light flicked on, and Greg and I darted our eyes toward the kitchen. Without looking at us, our host friend opened the refrigerator. Greg and I stopped, frozen, and he tried to unravel himself from under my shirt and I quietly tried to refasten his belt. Closing the refrigerator door, moving back toward his bedroom without looking at us in the living room, Greg and I thought we were somehow undiscovered in the dark living room, only lit dimly by the sun peeking through the curtains.

We exhaled in relief, having been holding our breaths for what seemed like an eternity. We began to kiss again, until we heard faintly from the hallway, "7 and 8, sitting in a tree...

Welcome Home

I drove home and slept until noon, the haze from the previous night's drunk finally lifted. I thought about Greg, and how amazing he'd made me feel. As much as I thought about wanting him, I forced myself not to contact him after I'd ran out of the apartment, leaving him standing alone in the living room.

Staring at the ceiling, I felt around for my phone and lifted it to my face, combing through text messages to make sure I hadn't sent anything stupid while drunk, and then made my way to my emails. There was one from Frank.

"CCC... can't wait to see you soon."

I closed my eyes, and tried to remember what day it was, when would I actually be seeing him again? I had promised to pick him up from the airport, but I'd completely forgotten what day his flight would be arriving. I filtered through my emails with urgency to find the flight itinerary he'd sent me. My eyes widened. Tomorrow. Frank was coming in tomorrow.

I shot out of bed, and headed toward the bathroom. I studied my reflection, wondering if I looked like someone who had just made out with someone else. Was there guilt in my eyes? Did I smell of another man? The idea dawned on me, and I immediately hopped in the shower, removing any physical remnants from last night. After a thorough cleansing, I studied myself again in the mirror.

There were no hickeys, no noticeable signs that another person had touched me in any way.

Frank was coming home tomorrow, I'd be picking him up. I'd be greeting him at the airport. This was the day I'd been looking forward to, the bleakness of my days strung together by the lack of him.

But last night, I'd had friends. I'd met people, I'd had a good time, someone had made me feel good. Did I need Frank as much as I thought I had? I felt like maybe all I'd really needed was a way to break up the monotony, and maybe even the things I'd told people I'd been doing.

Maybe I would start running, doing yoga, and reading... what was stopping me from becoming the person I'd told people I was? I'd felt the person who'd been fading, disappearing from me come to life, as I'd imagined the life I could have, the person I could be.

The following day, I'd swung by Frank's house for the first time since he left, doing a little sweep to ensure there were no break ins or anything fishy for him to come home to. Then, I headed toward the airport. I waited in the cell phone lot, figuring that being early was better than keeping Frank waiting. Seeing Frank's name pop up as a text message for the first time in a month invoked an unplaced feeling.

This was the day I'd been waiting for, and here it was, and I'd felt nothing. Although, that wasn't necessarily true. It was almost as though I had been waiting for Frank to leave all while I was with him, yet when he was gone, I'd realized that my days, my life, everything was lacking so much without him. Maybe I needed him to be gone for a long period of time while I discovered what I'd lost by having him in my life. I could train myself to be more like him, to be satisfied with a little smiley face or a short exchange before returning to my adventure, my own wonderment.

I pulled up to the curb, seeing Frank waiting with his giant baggage and briefcase. I turned off my car to help him load things into the trunk, and off we were. Since we were in public, and in a hurried environment, we didn't greet each other with a hug or anything other than a verbal exchange. As we drove on, I'd wondered what we'd looked like to bystanders.

Would people think I was his daughter? No, they couldn't, right? Whenever I'd seen young adults picking up their parents from the airport, they always exclaimed, or seemed thrilled, and they almost always said "mom" or "dad" in their exclamations. Would people have known that we were somehow romantically linked? That was possible, despite the obvious age difference, however I felt as though the embrace, some kind of physicality would be involved in the greeting. Perhaps, instead, I seemed like his driver, or his assistant.

A degree of intimacy removed, a transactional sort of relationship.

Arriving at his home, we unloaded the car and I helped him in through the front door. He glanced around sadly.

"You didn't stay here at all, did you?"

I wasn't quite sure how he would have known that, just by the looks of it. Although undisturbed, I wouldn't have left the place in shambles had I stayed over at all, so I was confused as to what sort of disarray he'd been hoping to find. Frank had looked hurt, as though all the while he was gone, he'd wanted his home lived in, he wanted to know I was here, living, breathing him.

"Well," I started, "I actually drove by just this morning. I didn't want you to come home to a break in, or something strange after a long trip."

Frank's face lightened, enjoying the idea of me thinking about him while he was gone. Little did he know, he was nearly all I thought about.

I let him unpack, shower, and relax while I pretended to have a lot to tell him. I mentioned friends coming, going, talking, drinking, and Frank seemed interested in my stories, not because of the content, but just to feel as though he were filled in to my life without him.

He laid on his bed next to me, and kissed me forcefully. He darted his tongue back and forth, and I remembered that the day before, I had kissed someone else, and I'd liked it.

I'd even thought I'd made a mistake, thinking it was really Frank that I craved, but now, because of this, I'd known that was decidedly not the case. I felt Frank fumble on top of me, while I allowed the aggression on my mouth. He began to put his fingers up my skirt, and thrust his fingers inside of my vagina. I yelped, which he took as a sign of encouragement, and kept moving his fingers in a circular motion. Then, he paused. He rose above me for a moment, his finger still inside of me.

"I have to tell you something."

I waited patiently, wondering what could be so important to interrupt what he thought was a good time.

"I don't like that you shave your vagina. I want you to be natural."

He wanted me to be natural. I nodded, not knowing what else to do, and he began kissing me again. I don't think he knew what being natural meant for me. I'm sure that no one really knew what that meant for me. I didn't think anyone would want it.

I felt his finger swirling uncomfortably inside of me, and in a split second, I pushed him off of me. He laid on the bed, startled, and I climbed on top of him, ripping my clothes off, and pawing at his shirt, which he unbuttoned and slipped off of himself. I unbuckled his belt, thinking about how only yesterday, I had gotten this far with Greg.

How different their belts had been, Greg's had been a bit cheap, flimsy, and yet necessary on his thin frame. Frank's thick, expensive, and used mainly out of habit. I tore off his pants, and leaned over him to kiss him, fully, on his mouth. Frank let me have control, and I began to rub my vagina over his penis, which flopped around unaffected as I'd become more and more wet.

I remembered how feeling Greg's erection pressed up against my stomach had made me burn for him, and suddenly, it was as though I were sitting in a puddle on Frank's pelvis. I closed my eyes, and began to grind on Frank, wishing I had done more with Greg, so I'd have more of a memory to go off of to make myself orgasm. Frank's penis did a weird flop, which ended up pinching my clitoris in a way that created a small, sharp euphoric pain, and I flinched, shuttered, and closed my eyes tighter.

I had been hospitalized for a period of time in my youth, and every week, nurses would need to check each inpatient's vital signs, which always included blood work. I'd dreaded this procedure most of all, as I'm sure the majority of people do. I would often get in my head about it, and start to feel nauseous and light-headed. There were multiple times when I'd fainted, or cried uncontrollably during getting my blood drawn, and I'd always held on to those moments in my head, building it up, becoming a self-fulfilling prophecy.

One week in particular, the clinic decided to have nurses-in-training attempt to take the patients' blood. The one nurse assigned to me looked particularly nervous, as she shakily grabbed my forearm, tightening the strap above my elbow. She told me to make a fist, and to open and close my hands as she tightly pressed my forearm.

"Your veins are so small…" she whispered.

I felt nauseous, and my ability to make a fist became grueling as all of my strength was focused on preventing me from toppling over.

"And you have floating veins."

My stomach lurched as she repeated the same lines most doctors and nurses did before drawing blood through immense difficulty, and I attempted to prepare myself for the worst. Which, whatever I thought the worst was before, was nowhere near as bad as it was going to be.

After minutes of multiple punctures, attempts that withdrew nothing but syringes of my sanity, the nurse suggested we try drawing blood from my foot.

"Feet have a lot of veins," she said, panicked. "We'll be able to get something from your feet."

Sweating profusely, I lifted my vibrating leg up to her, allowing her to stab my foot in a way that sent unusual pangs through my body. My eyes closed, I'd assumed she must have gotten some amount of my blood, but the silence was then interrupted by her quivering voice.

"I'm... I'm so sorry. We, we have to go back to your arm."

My eyes shot open, and I glared at her, pleading, with tears in my eyes.

"I know, I know...." She begged. "I'm so sorry, this will be it."

I swung my leg back down, a sharp pain shooting through my calf. I winced, and dejectedly laid my left forearm across the table once more. She quickly started to rub the pit of my elbow, feeling for the places she'd already penetrated. I kept my eyes closed, feeling the circular movements of her thumb on my forearm, the rhythmic motions felt almost like a massage.

I let myself feel at ease, relaxed in her grip. She rubbed me in short, slower strokes, back and forth. I knew this couldn't last forever, but I let myself enjoy it, and a moment later, she whispered again.

"I'm so sorry."

And before I could register what was about to happen, the nurse slipped the needle into my forearm, twisted, and popped a vein. I let out a glass-shattering scream, my eyes opened to see a vial of blood, sloppily filled as the butcher across from me frantically tried to remove the needle from my arm.

I had never seen such a dark bruise surface so quickly, a tennis ball shaped shadow cast on the afflicted area of my forearm. I started sobbing, only inhaling to prevent myself from vomiting. The nurse could only wrap up the puncture, and continuously apologize as I limped out of the office, clutching my arm, sobbing.

I opened my eyes, and allowed my face to serenely drift from the ceiling to meet Frank's face.

"Wow," he sighed. "That looked like it felt really good."

Leaving Again

Two weeks flew by, and just like that, it was time for Frank to set off on his next trip, heading to Michigan for a month. I found the two weeks to be cheerful, knowing that our time together was fleeting, and precious before he left again. I was still uncertain as to why I had enjoyed his company much more than usual.

Had I realized what we had together, how much I'd wanted and needed him in my life since he'd been gone? Or had I simply just known that he'd be leaving soon, and I'd be free of him again? We'd spent nearly every day together, chatting, cooking, and my days felt so vibrant, so colorful with him. I couldn't imagine why I had ever found him repulsive, why I'd ever had anger or resentment bubble up toward him.

There was nothing wrong with him, his kindness and affections pouring and radiating out of him. This, he brought and took with him everywhere he went, it surrounded and permeated his person. His house always felt so clean, fresh, and the tidiness had made me feel as though I were staying in a hotel, our life together a vacation. I would only go home to shower and change, never quite being honest with myself about spending the night or how long I would stay over, thus never packing a bag or preparing to stay for more than a day.

My own apartment seemed so dark, and although not unkempt, it was not as inviting as Frank's home. I felt as though I couldn't get myself out of my own place fast enough.

Even as we were spending as much time together as we were, Frank and I would still exchange emails, messages, in his very Frank-fashion. In every way, we were connected. He seeped his way into every aspect of my life, twisting and winding into my thoughts and personality. I felt myself wanting to be smarter, better, more like him. I'd even bring work from my internship over to his home, so he could see me being productive, studious.

He would write, too, and we would discuss what we'd be eating for dinner and other simple, domestic things across the room from each other from where we worked separately. Until, eventually, the conversations became about his upcoming departure. I had promised to take him to the airport this time, and I found discussions about him leaving starting to unsettle me.

Our life finally seemed to be coming together, and I didn't want to lose the stability that we had created. I knew it was passing, and too good to be true.

Our last evening together, we finally finished the second half of the movie we started, watching the main characters' relationship dissolve from the comfort of the couch. One of the characters had cheated on the other and was found out.

"You suck his dick, then you come home and kiss me on the mouth?"

There was a slap. Lots of crying. Shoving.

After the movie, Frank and I discussed what we'd have done in that situation, and the concept of cheating.

"I think I'd have responded in the same way. I completely agree, I'd hate the feeling that someone else had had the person I love right before I did," considered Frank.

That sounded territorial to me, although I had understood what he meant. I didn't like the idea that he would feel as though his significant other had been tarnished, or sullied by another person. The trust would of course be lost, and the relationship may or may not be salvageable, but I did think that was up to the couple to determine.

"For example, if you cheated on me, Rin, I'd feel terrible."

My stomach burned as I remembered kissing Greg, and my face felt red, hot. Frank noticed, and cocked his head inquisitively. I had to act fast.

"Well, technically I can't cheat on you. I'm not your girlfriend."

Frank's eyes relaxed, and he laughed curiously. He didn't suspect a thing.

"You don't think we're in a relationship? Catherine, you're here every day. We sleep together, we do everything together. I love you. Isn't that enough of a relationship for you?"

"Well, we never had a conversation about it. I had told you I didn't really want to be in one. There needs to be some sort of agreement, right? I would never just assume I'm in a relationship with someone."

Frank considered and nodded.

"Okay, fine. Do you want to be in a relationship?"

A few years prior, I had been sleeping with someone for a few months, satisfied with the lack of labels and the ambiguity of the arrangement. The only reason the discussion of a relationship arose was because someone else had referred to me as this guy's girlfriend, and my head whipped toward him. I wasn't able to contain my shock.

"Girlfriend?"

He was unfazed.

"Well, do you want to be?"

I looked away from him, staring straight ahead, and then turned to face him, and offered my hand. I thought it would be funny to shake on it, to make it official, but as it turned out, it was confusing and unclear. He thought I was rejecting him politely, and we went on in our routine, me thinking we were in a relationship and he thinking that I'd still wanted to sleep with him. It wasn't until a random discussion months later that the terms of our relationship were clarified.

Frank and I were essentially in a relationship already, like it or not, and whether or not I'd stopped to think about what we'd been doing. It wasn't that I disliked the idea of our relationship, but I hated that I had committed to something without even realizing.

I looked at Frank and smiled. He seemed to understand.

After dropping Frank off at the airport the next day, I had decided to return to his house instead of my own, thinking that unwinding in his crisp, sunny living room would be clearly superior to moping in my lonely apartment.

Pulling up to his house, I finally got to use the second set of keys, and opening the front door, I was greeted with the familiar room that I'd been in only hours before. The room hours ago had been lively, happy, but where I stood, it felt empty. I felt empty. The living room had the same shadowy feeling that my apartment had, the ceaseless and unshakable feeling of despair.

    I walked to the fridge to grab a beer, seeing the leftover macaroni and cheese Frank and I had made together. I sighed, sitting on the couch, staring at the drawn curtains over his picture window. I sat in silence, in the dark. I could have pulled the curtains, to let in the light, or even just flip a god damn switch to turn a light on, but I didn't. I sat, alone.

    This living room had been buoyant with Frank, yet his absence seemed to zap all the life out of it. All the room had now was me, who I am. That's all any room had to look forward to. Guests to welcome and the warmth each presence would bring. Deep down, I knew why I couldn't bear to be in my apartment by myself anymore, why each day had been brighter because of Frank. I'd known that no matter where I went, no matter which room I sat in, the same sinking feeling would follow me.

Intermission

"There's no way you haven't slept with anyone else. There's just no way. You couldn't. It's been six months, you couldn't have waited that long without fucking someone else."

This statement, this almost question was entirely unprompted, no conversation inviting this assumption. Laying on my back, I remained still, quiet. I stared up at the ceiling as he waited for me to respond. I felt his eyes on me, and from my peripheral vision, I could see his bare chest still heaving as he had himself propped up on a forearm, facing me.

Both of us were still naked. But still I stayed, staring ahead, and I let myself smile. He knew that I didn't have to answer, though, and more than that, that I wouldn't. I knew he wanted me to tell him whether or not I'd slept with anyone else since the last time he and I had, thinking that, even though we weren't anything in particular, that I was his nothing in particular.

Whenever he'd try to ask me questions like these passively, or subtly, I chose to ignore them. Even on the off chance he'd ask me a direct question, I'd usually shoot him a look that conveyed that I was sparing him the details, and that I was making the executive decision not to tell him the truth. To this, he'd drop his inquiries, and we'd get back to not talking.

Austin and I met the summer before, as he'd worked in the financial aid office at the university, and I was having issues with said financial aid. Austin would sometimes email me, which I wouldn't see until after I returned home, or he'd call the number on file, which happened to be my mother's house phone. The subsequent game of phone tag would drive me over the edge, and my mother would reassuringly say that he did genuinely sound sorry for the phone tag and back and forth.

There had been days when I'd have to go to the office four times in order to fill out a form, or to sign a line I'd overseen, and eventually, out of sheer frustration, I stormed into the office.

"Here's my phone number. Just call or text me."

And so, he did.

We'd been sleeping together casually since that summer, at first testing the waters for potentially dating, but after a while, we both knew that we weren't what the other was looking for. The sex, however was pretty decent, and I was perfectly willing to carve out time to drive up to see him once a week or so, until things sort of tapered off.

To be fair, the sex was almost entirely decent because of his dick, but he'd never made any attempts to actually make me orgasm. I'd always faked it, just to have a secret. It had very little to do with inflating his ego, but more so that I could have something to hide. I wasn't sure why I needed that. We were already hiding each other.

Austin had texted me at the party I had been at a few weeks ago, which was a good starting point for a conversation, since he'd invited me to stay the night and I didn't want to be home alone. Being alone with him was always a chore, and even though we never quite knew where to start a conversation because we had so many differences, we also had no trouble keeping the conversation going once we got started.

Since we hadn't seen each other in a long time, we'd had a lot more to discuss than we normally had. He asked me about my Scholar's Day speech, in which I gave a presentation about a study of mathematics called rubber sheet geometry. Austin had also majored in mathematics four years before me, and actually used to attend the same university, nabbing a job in the same office he'd done his work study in right after graduation. He was also working on his masters degree. I thought about how strange his resume must have looked.

A love letter to the school.

We started to slowly reveal what each of us had been up to that summer, I gave him my rehearsed summer spiel, tactically leaving out anything about Frank. I found myself wanting to talk about Frank, though. I wanted to find ways to weave him casually into a conversation, my head so consumed with him. As though he were acquiescing to my desires, Austin was detailing working over the summer, how empty the campus is, especially the staff and faculty parking lot.

"I especially miss Dr. Joyce. He and I both have Subarus and we only drive manual. The school year is fun because we always try to park right next to each other, chat about cars. The campus is a fucking ghost town."

My ears perked up at the mention of Frank, and I jumped at the opportunity to talk about him as long as possible.

"It must be hard for you, because he usually teaches summer school, right? But I guess this summer has taken him elsewhere."

Austin didn't seem at all suspicious, knowing that Frank had been the type of professor everyone loved and talked about.

"Yeah, that's true! I hadn't thought about that before, but yeah. Last year, he'd been around campus a bit more than this year. I miss that guy. It's always weird to see him outside of school, though. I remember once, I saw him at my buddy's graduation party, and he was drinking from the keg. I don't know. Don't you think it's weird to see professors and teachers outside of the context in which you know them?"

I let a laugh escape me, thinking about how many places I'd seen Frank during this summer alone. I'd seen him in my car, walking into an airport. I'd seen him cooking in his kitchen, I'd seen him at a strip club. I'd seen him in his bedroom. I looked at Austin and wondered how he'd react if he knew that he and Frank had both been inside of me, how out of the context in which he knows Frank that would be to him.

"I suppose so."

The conversation had actually not made me feel more uncomfortable about seeing Frank in these many places, and had inspired me to want to see him in even more. I leaned over Austin, my bare breast rubbing against his chest, to grab my phone. Ignoring Austin's inquisitorial eyes, I began to text Frank, carefully angling my phone so that Austin wouldn't be able to see exactly what I had been doing.

"See you in Michigan?"

I placed the phone on the other side of me, away from Austin, and looked back at him, pretending we hadn't skipped a beat.

"So, how's grad school going?"

As he bitched and moaned about his course load, I started to fantasize about visiting Frank in Michigan. Was that message too forward? How would he react to it? I'd hoped his heart would flutter, enrapturing him. I imagined us in Michigan, him at a library, studying, and me with a laptop, still pretending to do research. Would I be able to be seen with him? Would he want me to sit with him in the library? There was so much potential, so much for us to do together.

I felt my phone vibrate from behind me, and without breaking eye contact with Austin, I reached around myself to feel around for it. Frank had responded.

"You're kidding. Don't play with me like that."

As Austin was still probably speaking, I lifted the phone to my face, blatantly ignoring him.

"When's good for you? I'm free this weekend."

I stared at my phone, knowing he was there on the other side, and I waited.

"I'll see it when I believe it…" Frank taunted.

Immediately, I interrupted Austin and ordered him to hand me my purse. Surprisingly, he obliged, shocked by my brazen behavior. I pulled out my wallet, scrambling for my credit card, while I began to book a flight for Detroit for the weekend. Finding the cheapest ticket, I impulse purchased a direct flight to Detroit for three days, three days from that moment. Riding the high of my whim, I took a screenshot of the reservation confirmation page, and sent it to Frank as a response to his jeer.

I dropped my phone on the bed in front of me, careful to ensure the screen was facing downward, and I put my wallet back into my bag and turned back around to Austin. He widened his eyes, beckoning an explanation, and I shrugged.

"I just bought a ticket to Michigan."

"You just did? Right now?" He said, completely aghast. "Well, honestly. I know you pretty well at this point. You don't really give a fuck and just do whatever you want. What are you going to do there?"

Frank. "Probably visit some friends there, we'll see. I haven't fully planned it. Actually, Austin, I'm going to head home. Text you later."

I rolled out of bed, and felt powerful, taking my time to put on my clothes, in a rush to leave but in no hurry to run out. I thoroughly relished the discomfort and disrespect I'd just created. I stole a glance at Austin, whose eyes seemed to say "you win".

I strutted out of his house, feeling victorious. All of the times Austin had commented about me gaining weight, or any unnecessarily critical comment he'd thrown at me carelessly, I'd felt I'd been able to reclaim my self-respect, in a way, by being the bigger asshole in our unspoken competition. My conscience was operating guilt-free, too, knowing that my decision to go out of my way to fuck Austin had been because I felt as though my feelings for Frank had gotten out of hand, and I disliked the inadvertent control over me he'd seized.

I knew it was never his intention, and that there was nothing malicious about his feelings for me, but my yearning for him was inexplicable, and it scared me how much of me he occupied. By fucking someone else, I could lie to myself that I hadn't actually cared that much about Frank, because then how could I do what I just did?

Arriving at my own apartment, I turned on the light and flopped down on the couch. I mooned over the possibilities of my trip to Michigan, feeling as though I could finally catch a glimpse of Frank's life. I romanticized Frank, yes, and everything he'd had, and I wanted a taste or more, as much as I could, and I felt like I was finding a way to skip ahead, foregoing the hard work and snatching these exciting moments, stealing them, taking what was not rightfully mine.

I laid back, thinking of all of the things I'd need to do before leaving. I'd need to tell Chloe I'd be leaving, but I couldn't possibly tell my parents. I didn't talk to my parents daily, so it would be easy for me to get away with a weekend trip without them knowing.

Like seeing Austin, like my entire relationship with Frank, like the majority of my seedy activities, this trip would be yet another secret. Thrilled with myself, my life, drunk with meaningless power, I tried to think of a good alibi for why I should have any reason to be in Michigan.

I combed through my contacts, remembering two of Chase's friends that I had gotten along with really well had also lived in Detroit. It was perfect. I could contact them, and say that I'd be visiting with my friends, and make time to meet up with them. It'd be the perfect scapegoat, if anyone found out I'd gone to Michigan. Satisfied, I texted my friends, and checked Frank's response.

"Catherine, Rin... There are so many things for us to do, see. I can't wait for you to be here with me."

I fell asleep on my couch, thoughts of Michigan and Frank swirling through my mind. I was intoxicated by the uncertainty of the future, undertakings unknown still in store, and more secrets and trophies for me to collect along the way.

Michigan

The subsequent days leading up to my departure were filled with excited exchanges between Frank and I. Frank willingly tasked himself with planning out the entire weekend, mapping out all of the sightseeing spots that we could realistically reach within three days. From what we'd be drinking, to what we'd been seeing, Frank had it under control. I just had to show up.

I told Frank that I'd need to make an effort for us to see my friends in Detroit, because it would be the perfect cover story for why I'd been in Michigan. My line of thinking impressed him.

"Huh. Good call. I wouldn't have thought about that."

It concerned me slightly that he hadn't thought about tying loose ends, and covering our trails, but fortunately doing things under peoples' noses was my strong suit.

I wore tight, high-waisted shorts, a ribbed, lace top with thigh high socks on my flight, wanting to wow Frank as soon as he picked me up from the airport. Arriving at Detroit Metro Airport Friday afternoon, my outfit garnered many blatant glares from nearly every person in arrivals.

I took a mental note of all of the university hoodies and sweatpants around me, and thought about how I must have looked to these people. I thought about Frank pulling up to the curb to pick me up in a rental, and imagined people craning their necks to see who would be coming to get the costumed young woman, and the assumptions they'd have when they saw my ride was a man twice my age. One of my friends texted to ask if my flight had arrived.

"Yes, and everyone is staring at me." I sent him a picture of my outfit. He called me, laughing.

"Yeah, you can't dress like that here. You gotta tone it down. Anyway, are you with your friend? Where is she?"

I hadn't said anything about Frank, only referring to him as my friend I'd be with in Michigan. They knew nothing of his gender, his age, our relationship. I thought it'd be funnier for my friends to be surprised when they finally met Frank. I told my friend we'd see each other on Sunday, and I'd hung up, spotted my suitcase, and headed toward the doors. I saw Frank within seconds, and charged right up to the car, knocking on the passenger side window to get his attention. He turned toward me slowly, and I motioned for him to unlock the backseat so I could throw my bags in the back without him needing to get out of the car to assist me.

I was mainly trying to withhold him from the nosey stares from outside.

First on our itinerary was to check out Lansing to walk around and grab some lunch. Walking around the city felt fresh, different. The city felt very sparse, and managed to feel too spread out despite its size. I sat down on a bench, enjoying the weather and the idea of being in a new place, my first time in this state. The city wasn't so bad, and I'd come into the scenario with no expectations, and thus, it didn't disappoint.

Frank took a seat next to me on the bench and asked what I thought.

"It's fine, cute. Quaint. I just want..." I looked around and gestured before me, "more?"

Frank laughed, and looking around at the city, nodded, and suggested we go find food.

We found a cute rooftop eatery. Perusing the menu, I found the food to be just out of touch with what I had been familiar with. There were dishes with names like "The Hillbilly Deluxe" and portions that seemed larger than my arm span. Each order was doused with gravy or whipped cream. What was the point of this food?

Did people want to feel absolutely sick to their stomachs after eating? Did people understand that food was for nourishment, not just for gluttonous pleasure? I looked at Frank, asking if most restaurants here were like this. He looked amused, and said that all of the restaurants he'd wanted to take me to were like this.

He'd always been the type of person who wanted to put people out of their comfort zones. Have them try new things. Even things like clogging their arteries.

I gave him a fake smile, and dove back into the menu, figuring there'd have to be something I could get away with ordering without looking like I was caving so early on in this trip. My eyes floated down each side of the menu and finally rested upon deep fried frog legs.

Remembering Frank sending me the photo of the woman butchering the frogs while he was abroad, I thought to myself that this would warrant a reaction. It wasn't a traditional order, and although it wasn't as healthy as I'd had liked, there didn't seem to be a single vegetable available on the menu unless it was sandwiched between two beef patties.

The waiter approached us, and right as he finished asking if we were ready, I ordered my frog legs and the waiter and I both looked at Frank at the same time. Frank, looking astonished, didn't take his eyes off of me while he ordered a double cheeseburger with a side of fries. The waiter thanked us and walked off, and Frank continued to stare at me in wonder.

I pretended not to notice, and looked back down at the table, grabbing my water and taking a swig before meeting his eyes again.

"What?" I asked, innocently.

"You just ordered frog legs. I just wasn't expecting that."

I could anticipate his next question.

"Did you do that... why did you do that?"

I saw this coming. He would be wondering if I'd ordered it on purpose to get his attention, to woo him, or if I just happened to have a hankering for frog legs. I knew what my true motives were, but I knew I couldn't tell him that I'd seen it and got it to impress him—and because frog legs were ironically the least disgusting sounding thing on the menu—because then any normal person with no ulterior motives would have pointed them out. They would have invited him into the know.

But I hadn't. I'd intentionally excluded him from why I'd wanted the frog legs because I wanted to see how he'd react, and he was far surpassing any expectations I'd imagined. I'd wanted to keep this going, to see what else I could get him to say, to feel.

"Oh! Yeah, I mean, it just seemed interesting. I've never seen it on any menu before, and I've never tried it before."

I could see Frank was unable to comprehend the flood of thoughts and emotions that seemed to overcome him.

"Don't you remember the photo I sent you, of the dead frogs, with all the blood?"

Bingo. "Oh! Oh wow, yeah! You did send that to me, for my birthday, right? Huh, what a curious coincidence. Well, I suppose we can say I'm eating my birthday dinner tonight."

Frank's wide eyes started to glaze over, a dullness coming about them. He didn't quite look like himself anymore, and I'd begun to worry I'd gone too far, played with him too much. The light returned to his eyes, and he looked back down at the table, sheepish about going somewhere else that I was all too familiar with. I asked him if he was okay.

"Yeah, just. Just wow."

Our dishes arrived, and I lifted a set of fried frog legs to my face, one leg in each hand, and I laughed as I showed Frank. He seemed positively trance-like, watching me, his head bobbing as though he were a snake, and I, his charmer. I reveled in this, finally knowing that aside from health and sustenance, there were other, more gluttonous, pleasurable reasons to order food.

We set off on our journey, headed to the Sleeping Bear Sand Dunes. We hoped to arrive by the evening, staying in a hotel and heading out to the actual dunes the following morning. We drove for hours, and I watched the Midwest fly by me in a stream of cars, billboards, and large expanses of outlet malls. I loved seeing the off-ramp signs, beckoning people with promises of gas and fast food. We sped by one that promised both Chipotle and Qdoba, and I wondered how both could stay in business with such close proximity to each other. I'd supposed all other chains were able to do so, nearly all of them within a stone's throw of another.

"Chipotle or Qdoba. Discuss."

I turned to face Frank, whose eyes were still ahead on the road. I laughed.

"You've clearly written too many test prompts in your life."

I remembered his classes, and his way of speaking, how he wrote his tests, and even his syllabi. He always managed to somehow balance professional intellectualism and a casual warmth. He didn't ever over-explain anything, build anything up to an unnecessary degree. He spoke succinctly, and perfectly. Anyone would know why those two particular chains were being compared, and the only command was just to discuss.

It was brilliant. He was brilliant.

I thought about how I would have posed that same question.

"There are many fast food restaurants across America, and despite overlap and superfluous offerings, they all manage to get by, thrive even. As you know, Chipotle and Qdoba have similar menus. In your opinion, which one is better, worse, how do they differ, how are they the same?"

Too wordy. Frank always spoke volumes without the bells and whistles, and I imagined his mind, organized, uncluttered, and compared it to my own, the exact opposite.

We reached our hotel and dragged out our small weekend bags as we made our way to the lobby. There was still a startling amount of light out at this point, and I had remembered reading that there were some places in Michigan that have sunsets after 9 pm in the summer.

It still felt as though we had so much time, though we'd been driving for hours. Frank had been highly excited by this room, though he kept much of it from me as a surprise. We were greeted by a friendly, middle-aged woman who had been expecting us.

"You must be Dr. Joyce!"

She checked us in, and asked if she could help us in any way.

"Yes, actually. Could you direct us to a restaurant or something around here? We haven't eaten dinner yet."

The woman politely began to list off restaurants, leaning over her counter to point out of the window in each of their respective directions.

"They close a bit early, though, so you might want to hurry. The other places are bars, which do serve food, but unfortunately, she won't be able to go because you have to be at least 21 to enter."

My face burned red, and I couldn't help but to defend myself.

"Oh, I am old enough. I'm actually 22."

The woman's face turned apologetic and she began to respond in kind, but then she caught herself, and looked up at Frank.

"Oh, she's not your daughter."

Her cheerful, customer-service façade dropped instantly.

"Well, that's about it. I'll show you to your room."

We walked in uncomfortable silence from the lobby, through the back pathway, which opened up to a vast, groomed garden, home to many little cottages. I tried to catch Frank's eye, but he seemed completely oblivious to the woman's obvious disapproval of us.

Beyond the garden, there was a view of Lake Michigan, which the sun was beginning to set lightly across. I'd never seen a lake that large, and felt as though it may as well have been an ocean. As far as I could see was water.

The pink and lavender woven into the fabric of the water, stitching upward to the sky made me feel so serene, so innocent. The woman showed us to our specific cottage, and opened the door for us. There was a single queen sized bed, which made her gasp in horror, and whip her head toward Frank, who stared ahead dreamily, as though still thinking about me ordering frog legs. She met my eyes, and I tried to smile, before looking down at the floor. She slammed the door key on the table nearest to the door, and stormed out without another word.

Frank and I stood in silence for a moment. My eyes burned.

"There's also a Jacuzzi in the back! But let's get some food first."

We went to one of the bars that served food, and I decided that I hadn't been hungry, and instead wanted to fill up on beer. Frank asked if I was sure I didn't want anything more substantial, but I'd felt a bit sick to my stomach and only wanted to fill myself up with forgetting.

I drank four beers on an empty stomach, while Frank ate his way through a basket of chicken wings. I thought about how I must have looked to that woman, who had sized me up at about 15 or 16 years old, taking a vacation with her father, and whose idea of my innocence must have been completely shattered by hearing my actual age, and seeing the one bed for Frank and I to share.

I felt very alone in this shame, as Frank either seemed not to notice, or didn't care. We walked outside, the sun still very much available, and made our way back to the cottage. I stole one more glance at the innocent lake, and headed inside.

Frank began to make us gin and tonics and he asked if we could go enjoy the hot tub. I grunted in agreement, unable to formulate coherent words, let alone full sentences.

"And Rin. I want to see you naked."

I took off my clothes obediently, hypnotized, and walked up to him, grabbing the gin and tonic he'd made me. I downed it in one gulp, and set it back down on the table. I asked for another and told him to meet me outside in the Jacuzzi.

I got the jets going, and decided to let myself slide in, my head rested against the edge. I stared up at the sky, noticing the soft pastels had dimmed to chalky, dark talc. Frank came to join me outside, naked, standing with a gin and tonic in each hand. I grabbed mine greedily and thanked him, and as he entered the Jacuzzi.

I began to feel my head spin. I stood up and sat on the edge, letting myself breathe. The light on the deck seemed like a spotlight on my body, making everything around me pitch black. I looked down at myself, slight, pale, my stomach flat from not eating dinner, following my thighs that were still dipped in the cauldron of bubbling water.

The swirling hues of innocence from earlier seemed obsolete, and all I could see now were the ingredients of reality. My leg stirring the pot of a toiling tonic, the steam bombarding my face. I stared down into the vat of gin, tonic, a sprig of rosemary, and frog legs. I inhaled the noxious fumes, every breath more labored and shallow. I hung my head over the water and closed my eyes, breathing into the potion of me.

TV Family

We took off early the next morning, and I waited outside of the lobby near the car having Frank deal with checking out on his own, too hungover and too embarrassed to meet the woman's judgmental gaze again.

We headed for the Sand Dunes, hoping to beat the afternoon sun, knowing all too well that it'd be a futile pursuit. By 10 am, the sun was already blazing, and I had to peel my face from the passenger side window to keep from getting a sunburn. I looked over at Frank, who'd been wearing sunglasses, driving quietly. I wasn't sure if he'd tried to talk to me at any point, or if we were on the same page of not talking. What happened last night?

I had felt myself get so drunk, had felt so out of control, and thus let myself get more out of control. I hadn't really remembered what had happened after being in the hot tub, or much of the night thereafter. I'd always hated confronting issues, but I knew we'd have to suffer through one more night together, and I didn't want to get too drunk again and let things get out of hand.

"How're you feeling?" I asked, vaguely.

Frank didn't take his eyes off the road. "Oh, not bad. I just didn't sleep very well."

His voice didn't seem at all irritated or spiteful, which didn't surprise me because I couldn't imagine that from him. His reaction didn't give me any clarity. I decided to press a bit further.

"Yeah, I'm sorry. I drank a lot last night, and I didn't really feel up for dinner. I don't really remember what happened. What happened in the hot tub?"

I could see Frank's eyebrows raise under his sunglasses, and he managed to steer his eyes off the road and toward me. He laughed in a reassuring way.

"Oh, no! You were fine. Really, it was kind of hot, actually. I could tell you weren't really yourself, though."

A burning feeling engulfed my stomach.

Staring down at my naked body, my skin looked slick, slimy. I felt repulsed staring at myself, and kept drinking, the fumes from the Jacuzzi mixing with my alcohol. My head was spinning, and I kept staring out into the darkness, avoiding looking down at my miry flesh.

"You look so beautiful in the moonlight,"

Furious, I stared at him, no word of reply. I sunk my body back down into the water, and looked back out into the abyss. How could he find me beautiful? I took another sip of my drink, and watched my body from above. The ripples from the jets distorted my body in a way that made me look wavy. How could someone look at me, and think I was beautiful, when I was clearly vile?

I couldn't stop thinking about the look the hotel clerk gave us, how her entire demeanor changed when she realized our relationship wasn't familial. How could someone who claimed to love me not see me for what I am? A childish, selfish little girl who is either taking advantage of an older man, or who is letting herself get taken advantage by an older man. I knew if it had to be one of the two it was the former, rather than the latter, but deep down I knew it was neither.

I knew that I had feelings for him in some capacity, that I enjoyed him somehow, but I didn't know if I could shake this dark feeling about myself.

I couldn't help but remain completely fixated on that woman, and what she thought of us. Was this all really worth it? I could handle the idea of him, the idea of us, when there was only us. Once we started to face the outside world, I wasn't sure I was ready to overcome how people made me feel, how I'd made me feel about what people thought.

Were my feelings for him strong enough to overlook everyone else?

His eyes stared at me thirstily, and I waded over toward him. If he thought I was beautiful, even when I hated myself, then maybe he could make me feel safe. We could work through any difficulty together.

Wait, no. If he couldn't see how much I'd hated myself right now, then maybe he didn't really understand the struggles we'd face. Did he even notice how that woman treated us? Would it be only me, facing the backlash of our relationship because his head was too far in the clouds to care?

My head was swimming with endless thoughts and alcohol, and I hadn't noticed that I'd stopped walking over to Frank. He was staring at me, concerned. I stood, refocusing my gaze, making no attempt to make any excuses for what must have looked like me vacating my body. Frank made his way toward me, and took the drink from my hand. I looked up at him, and he brought his face down towards mine to kiss me.

I wasn't sure if he was trying to be reassuring, or sexual. I didn't feel like that was the proper response to seeing me so drunk, so sad. I decided that if this is what he wanted, who he found beautiful, then I'd show him what he'd signed up for. I began to kiss him back a bit more aggressively, and he began to follow my lead.

I walked him backward to his respective seat, and pressed him down, his arms slung back over the ledge of the hot tub. I straddled him, my naked body pressed against him. My nipples were hard, tickled by his chest and I snaked my tongue further into his mouth, writhing my slippery body all over his. I thought about all of the times he kissed me with his burrowing tongue, the times he covered me in lube, and realized this is exactly what he wanted.

The rest of the drive was a blur, and even when we arrived at the Sand Dunes, I felt as though I couldn't get far enough away from him. Luckily, there was an abundance of space, the desert and sand neverending. He seemed more interested in taking photos of me from afar than actually being next to me.

I saw families together, little children running in the sand, while their parents laughed and took pictures. I sighed, feeling like we either looked like them, or we looked like something far more unacceptable. I placed my bag on the ground, and laid my head on top of it, staring up at the sky. My head was still throbbing from my hangover, but I willingly exacerbated the pain so I wouldn't have to think about anything else. I let the searing persist for a few minutes, until a shadow fell upon my face. I looked up, seeing Frank standing above me.

"Hey," he laughed. "I just took a picture of that family over there. They asked me to."

He gestured toward the family with the rabid children.

"They asked if we wanted to take a picture together. What do you think?"

I peered behind Frank's feet, and in the distance, I saw a man and a woman waving toward me. I looked up at him.

"How did they know we were together?"

Frank's face fell, but his smile persisted.

"Well, they saw me taking photos of you from afar. That's why they came up to me to begin with, because they saw me already taking photos. Then, when we finished, they asked if I wanted a photo with you."

I looked back at the couple, who were talking a bit more hushed amongst themselves, continuing to steal glances back at us to see if we were watching. Had they thought he was someone creepy, taking photos of me? Had they approached him, thinking they'd have him cornered once they mentioned me, and he'd sheepishly decline? Now, I'm sure that family felt a little uncomfortable, knowing there was no bluff to be called, that he did in fact know me.

Before, they didn't know what to make of him, but now they didn't know what to make of us. Of me. I stood up, wincing from the pain in my head, and used my hand as a visor to cover my eyes. I waved back at the couple, and shook my head while smiling, politely declining their offer. Frank looked disappointed.

"Let's get the fuck out of here," I mumbled.

I started toward the car without waiting for his reply.

We didn't talk the entire rest of the way back to Detroit. I rested my face against the window, despite the blazing heat, pretending to be asleep.

We pulled into the parking lot of our hotel casino in the city, and my anger dissipated, checking my phone and remembering that we'd be meeting up with my friends later. I jumped out of the car, and eagerly snatched my bag from the back seat, storming in toward the lobby. Frank quickly grabbed his bag. He followed behind me closely, catching up quickly, his strides nearly doubling mine.

After checking in and throwing our bags onto one of the beds, I turned to Frank and asked if he was ready. My friends were already waiting for us at a bar nearby. Frank was searching my face for any tell of what was going through my mind, any reason as to why I'd been so frantic and upset all day. His query was met with feigned distraction, as I walked to the door, only turning back around to ask if he'd be coming.

Pulling up to the bar, my heart lifted. I could see my friends seated through the window, and suddenly wanted to open the door while Frank was still driving and run out to them. I began to unfasten my seatbelt before the car stopped, and as soon as the engine was off, I was outside of the car.

Frank struggled to get out of the car, and I rolled my eyes at him. I hated him for being old, for holding me back. When I'd arrived in Michigan, I'd thought it would be funny to see the look of shock on my friends' faces when they saw I'd come to Michigan to be with a man twice my senior, but after a couple of days of judgment and bewilderment, I didn't think I could face any more damning looks or comments. Leaning up against the car, I quickly pulled out my phone to warn my friends.

"My friend is old. Actually, he's my professor."

As soon as Frank managed to find his footing outside of the car, I set off toward the bar. I burst in through the doors, my arms wide as though I'd been walking into the colosseum as a gladiator. My friends were two large, muscular men who'd served in the military and whom I'd met through Chase. They yelled in astonishment, and we ran toward each other and embraced in a group hug. In the huddle, I asked in a whisper if they got my text, to which they said yes and asked what was going on.

Frank walked in, and we regretfully broke apart from our hug, and each of my friends went up to Frank to introduce themselves and shake hands. Surprisingly, my friends didn't make any sarcastic comments and held their composure far better than I would have imagined. We took a seat at the table my friends had already been waiting at, and then Frank excused himself to go to the restroom. As soon as he walked away, my friends began to hound me with questions.

"Dude, what the fuck? When did you start fucking your professor?"

"And how old is he?"

"Was this happening while we were there?"

Their questions came in such rapid succession that I barely had time to respond, especially around my laughing. I was only able to manage to answer that this had been a recent development, starting since the beginning of summer, well after they left. I motioned my head toward the restroom from which Frank was returning, and my friends got the hint to change the subject.

They amiably included Frank in their new line of questioning.

"So, what have you guys done in Michigan?"

I started talking about Lake Michigan, and the Sleeping Bear Sand Dunes, and my friends' eyes lit up in surprise.

"Wow, you really both did everything!"

It was funny to see my friends, who'd run drunkenly through the streets, who'd tried to start fights with bushes and trash cans outside of bars, gather themselves and play along with my charade.

"So, you were both in the military? Were you ever stationed in the Middle East?" Frank asked.

My friends excitedly began to regale stories of their camps being bombed, and I watched Frank's face as my friends' façade slowly started to fade away.

"Well, I mean, first thing you do when you hear the bombs—they train you to prepare, so we were totally ready—is to check your dick. Make sure your dick didn't blow clean off, because then otherwise, what's the point of living anyway?"

"Actually, first I checked my legs hadn't been blown off, then I checked my dick. If my dick is there, that's all well and good, but if I can't run, where am I gonna go with my dick? What's the point?"

Laughing to the point of tears while my friends carried on like this, back and forth, Frank stared in amusement, making no comments, just simply watching my friends get carried away with themselves. I could have stayed there forever, reminiscing with friends, Frank sitting there silently, admiring. I decided my friends and I needed a photo together—proof of my alibi for visiting Michigan—and then we hugged, and parted ways.

The happiness of seeing my friends lingered, and made Frank's existence more tolerable, even when he began to speak.

"Your friends are hilarious. They seriously sound like characters on a TV show. Do your friends all talk like that?"

I thought about my friends ragging on each other, the constant banter, nicknames, the inside jokes, the bickering. We did all really talk like that.

"Well, it's amazing. I couldn't believe how quick witted you all were. It was seriously like watching some TV family sitcom."

I thought of the four of us, sitting at the table together, my two friends, arguing over something childish like brothers, and Frank as the father beaming at them proudly from across the table. Where did that leave me? As the mother, I would have made them stop fighting. As a sister, I would have complained about them, or joined in on the fun. Didn't I, though? I suppose I just sat there, laughing, for the most part. Jeering at the TV, provoking the characters from the sideline. At any point, I knew things could have carried on without me. The dialogue, the characters exactly the same had I just walked outside and stared at them through the window.

Let Sleeping Bears Lie

Frank and I drove back to the hotel, and despite the gloom that I'd settled into, I found myself still in high spirits. It felt nice to reconnect with friends again, and it was also reassuring that my friends who are normally uninhibited, undaunted by social niceties, were able to hold it together and treat Frank and I as normal people. At least, to our faces.

I sunk back into the passenger seat, relieved by the interaction. The rest of society might have their opinions about us, but perhaps those who love us would be supportive of our relationship. I felt reassured knowing that not every interaction from the outside world involving Frank and I would be greeted with judgment and concern.

Arriving back at our hotel, Frank decided to do a little gambling while I headed upstairs to the hotel room. As much as my hatred and resentment from him had lightened, I still felt like I wanted some alone time to decompress.

Our hotel room had one large picture window that took up the entirety of the wall. I grabbed the curtains and moved them slowly back and forth, never having pulled curtains that took up so much area. The curtains were thick, and heavy, with a cape-like quality to them. I swayed them back and forth, rippling them along the window.

The summer after my first year of university, I continued to work my part-time job, happy to have an excuse to be out of the house after transitioning from the freedom of the dorms to the regressive parental house rules. Working in food service allowed me the ability to say I'd be working a late event, while going off to parties and attending other gatherings that I'd otherwise be questioned endlessly about.

During that summer, our kitchens were incredibly overwhelmed by chefs rage-quitting, or getting fired, and overall inability to operate efficiently. The events kept compiling, and the show had to go on, which forced the company to ask for another chef to come in from Portland in order to help facilitate smoother business decisions in the kitchens.

My coworkers were terrified of him. The first time I met him, I was in the event room, waiting for the chefs to bring the chafers down from the kitchens. While setting up the buffet table, I heard an impossible string of profanities, barking of orders, growing nearer. A line of chefs with shocked, broken faces rounded the corner, each carrying a chafer or platter of food, looking like sled dogs being guided by their musher urging them on from the back.

After each chef handed me an item, their faces toward the floor, looking dejected, they each scurried out of the room. I scrambled to put each food item in its rightful place, following the order of the set menu, and when I had but one dish left, I looked up and saw him standing in front of me, holding out his chafer in offering.

I looked up at his face, his eyes comically enlarged by the lenses of his glasses, his sharp jawline, his gangly body swimming in his chefs' coat. More than anything, though, was how he double-took when he saw my face, handed me the chafer, and said hi as a devious smile spread across his face. I almost dropped the chafer he handed me.

For a couple of weeks, I'd see him sporadically, and we'd exchange little glances, until one day, we were smoking cigarettes together outside, and he asked what I was doing later.

Knowing that I wouldn't have to be home at any specific time, I admitted that I'd had nothing going on, which welcomed an invitation to his hotel room later that evening. I quickly accepted, and he told me the hotel, the room number, and to just knock when I got there.

My chest was pumping, hot with excitement. I knew I shouldn't be doing what I was about to, but the secret in and of itself was exhilarating. Coupled with the fact that I had no idea what he wanted from me, or what was going to happen.

And the way he looked at me. I loved how he'd seem so angry, so full of hatred toward everyone around him, but his face seemed to soften without fail once he saw me. It made me feel unique, as though I could pacify him, as though I were beautiful enough to quell anger, war.

I drove to his hotel, walked past the concierge, and quickly found his hotel room. I didn't give myself enough time to think, or process anything, or breathe before forcing my fist to pound on the door. After quick stirring, I heard footsteps approach, and slowly, the door opened, and I was welcomed inside.

The evening was as innocent as a 19 year old visiting a 30 year old's hotel room could be, where we exchanged pleasantries—his real name being Robert—and we discussed our lives, my major, his career and life. Robert told me about his wife, and how they'd been together since college, following up with asking if I had a boyfriend. I had, at the time, been dating someone since the beginning of the previous school year.

"How'd you meet?" Robert asked, simply, and I went into great detail about the first time I'd seen my boyfriend, and how I thought he was the most handsome person I'd ever seen in my life. I'd happened to be friends with his roommate, and we hung out a few times and eventually started dating.

Robert considered my story. "I think that's always important to cherish that thought… the way he made you feel the first time you saw him. That's truly special, there aren't many moments like that in life."

Robert offered me a beer from his mini-fridge, and we laid on separate hotel beds and chatted until I felt it was best for me to head home. He walked me outside, thanked me for coming over, and I drove home, surprised by how things had played out, yet unsure of what I'd expected to happen.

Every few days, I'd find myself knocking on Robert's hotel door. I wondered if the concierge desk recognized me, seeing as I had never checked in, and almost always came during the evenings. Did they think I was a call girl? That'd be interesting. Did that particular hotel get a lot of call girls? Did the hotel even know about it? Did they even care? I probably didn't fit the bill, arriving usually in my work clothes from earlier in the day, or occasionally in normal, casual clothes when I'd swing by on a day off.

Eventually, the separate beds became us on one when he'd made an excuse to sit next to me. Clutching my beer in one hand, I inched myself over to make some room for him on my bed. I slunk up toward the headboard, and positioned myself upright to get a better look at what was in front of me. I brought one knee up to my chest, letting the other closest to him stay stretched out long, touching his when he'd shift or move closer to me. Robert continued our discussion as though he hadn't just bridged an entire gap between us, and I stared at him, considering his motives.

He had been upfront about being married, and asked me about being in a relationship as well. I didn't know for sure if he'd actually wanted anything else from me. Even if he did, I didn't quite understand why he'd been so forthcoming in talking about his wife, seemingly every detail on the table. Did it make him feel better that I was also in a relationship?

Granted, the stakes were far less high for me, but perhaps knowing two people were doing something wrong would essentially ensure the secret between us be kept. Had he thought that through? If I had started to develop feelings for him, and I wanted to break him and his wife apart, that'd be far more earth-shattering than my boyfriend finding out about me lurking in hotel rooms a few times a week with a married man.

I suddenly felt powerful, as though I had not only a secret, and the excitement, but also the upper hand.

I slid my upper body forward, keeping my lower back against the headboard. I looked knowingly at Robert, who appeared to be a little more flirty, and confident in the eye contact I was giving him. Robert set his beer down on the bedside table, and turned his torso to face me. With both hands, he grabbed my face and lifted mine up toward his. I stared into his magnified eyes, and watched as he bit his lips before pressing them fully into mine.

His mouth was strong and hungry for me. Robert's tongue slid in and out of my mouth, sometimes catching my tongue, or otherwise taking as much of me in as he could. I whimpered, my chest heaving up and down, and I fought between his mouth to inhale as much as possible. I wanted to have him inside of me, to have him be a part of me, to have more of him in me. I slowly positioned myself on top of him, and placed my beer can next to his. I climbed on top of his lap, and started kissing him more fully, more intentionally. I felt him rise and press into me, which only made me want him more. I moaned, and began to massage between his legs. Letting out a surprised groan, Robert grabbed my hands to stop me.

"Please, I haven't slept with anyone else in ten years. I wouldn't last a second."

Embarrassed, I pulled back, and began to dismount him. Robert, sensing my rejection, grabbed my thighs to keep me in place.

"It's not that I don't want to..." he started. "It's just that it won't be very good. I feel like it wouldn't be satisfying at all for you, and I'd be mortified, and what would we get out of it? Just knowing we crossed that threshold just to cross it?"

I nodded. If it wasn't even going to be pleasurable, why do it? Why did I want to take it all the way? Is that what I needed to make this all real to me? To have this secret connecting me to reality? Did I need physical proof that something had taken place with me?

Robert moved his face toward mine, nudging me to keep kissing him. I sunk further down into his lap, grabbed the back of his head, and kissed him passionately. He moved slowly on top of me, maneuvering me underneath him, as he thrust himself against me. I breathed deeply, moaning, my breath catching at uneven moments. Robert paused, closing his eyes, and swore quietly, before saying he was about to ejaculate.

"Is that okay?" He asked, rushed, and I nodded.

He brought himself up, kneeling in front of my face, and pulled out his throbbing penis, which I guided aptly into my mouth. I began bobbing my head, working my tongue around, and in no time, he had filled my mouth, groaning and grunting to completion. I swallowed, and patted the corners of my mouth with my hands. I looked up at Robert, uncertain of how to proceed next.

"Well, I guess it's your turn now."

Still on his knees above me, Robert began to remove my pants, and brought his face between my legs.

"My god, this is a gorgeous pussy."

My thighs began to quiver, and I watched him bury his face into me, his eyes closed, looking as though he were eating for the first time in weeks. He flicked his tongue, moving it pointedly and fully in all the right directions. Building with haste, I came almost unexpectedly, unaware of how loud I was. I laid in the bed, my chest visibly pounding, and Robert came to lay next to me.

We continued to kiss on our sides until I felt I should start heading home. I shyly grabbed my pants and started to get dressed, when I noticed Robert walking toward the window.

"Shit. I forgot we're on the first floor. I left the window open. Literally anyone could have seen that."

The reality of what we were doing, the secret, and how we'd both had something to lose had we been discovered, zapped all of the fun, the romance out of the room. Even though the damage was done, Robert ripped the curtains closed, swearing aggressively once more.

"Having fun?"

My thoughts were interrupted by Frank having entered the room. I blushed, not knowing fully how long he'd been standing there watching me, nor how long I'd been standing there, lost in thought. I composed myself and flung the curtains wide open, staring down at the stories beneath me. The heat emanating from my face was cooling off pressed up against the window, and I began to roll my face against it, massaging the ache from my head.

The light from the window cast an eerily uplifting glow. Despite how late it was, the sun itself hadn't completely gone down.

"Oh, just messing around," I lied.

Frank excused himself to the shower, and I sat on the bed, staring out of the picture window. From up here, no one could look into the room and see Frank and I, yet we'd been out in the world. We'd been seen, been discovered. We were approaching a place of no return, where we'd been able to operate at a decent capacity when no one was watching. But wait, hadn't my friends showed me it was possible for people to be understanding, to look past it? There was no way to know for sure but to keep trying, pressing onward. I didn't know what to expect, or even what I wanted, but I knew that I would always be willing to look behind a new curtain to find out.

Frank came out of the shower, and slumped down on the bed.

"You've got an early flight, CCC. Let's try to get some rest. What do you think? Curtains open or closed?"

"May as well keep them open."

I woke up early the next morning, my arm around Frank. We were both facing the massive window, and I saw the most gorgeous scene through the curtainless view. I tapped Frank's arm to slowly wake him up, and whispered into his face.

"Look at the sunrise. Isn't it beautiful?"

Falling Downstairs

I returned home only a week before Frank, my outlook on the relationship slightly more positive than it had been for the majority of the Michigan excursion. The week leading up to his arrival wasn't something I'd dreaded or longed for, like before.

There was a calmness, an acceptance and I'd felt for the first time in a long time that I wasn't adding pressure to the situation. I was just going to take each moment as it came, and deal with it as it happened. This newer outlook on the world, on us, allowed my mind for the first time in a long time to be at ease.

I picked Frank up from the airport, making a "long time no see" joke, as we sped off back to his house. He was relieved to be home, and I helped him carry his bags up the stairs so that he could take a much-awaited shower. I plopped myself on his bed, waiting for him to finish up. It was late in the afternoon, and I'd wondered what we'd be doing for the rest of the day, what he'd feel up to.

Hearing the shower water stop, I didn't readjust myself, but continued to stare straight up at the ceiling. Out of my peripheral vision, I could see Frank standing in the doorway to his bathroom, staring at me, watching me watch the ceiling. I wanted him to be able to get dressed in peace, to give him the privacy I would have wanted, but he seemed to want me to look at him. I tilted my head to the side, and met his eyes.

Frank had his towel wrapped around his waist, and I noticed that he'd lost some more weight while he was in Michigan. I felt like his weight seemed to fluctuate so much, that every time I saw him, every time he left and came back, he was a new person, or a different version of himself. I smiled at him, and he started toward me on the bed, crawling before he grabbed my face to bring it up to his. I let him kiss me, unbothered by the sloppiness, the fact that he thought he was doing a good job. I just let him be what he wanted to be to me.

Frank had decided he wanted sushi for dinner. The Midwest wasn't necessarily known for its stellar Asian cuisine, he said, so he called in for takeout from a place down the street. The restaurant said it'd take about two hours, since they were currently slammed during a dinner rush. Frank wanted to fix us some drinks before dinner, so we decided then to head downstairs.

Frank, in front of me, was walking abnormally fast for himself, and I watched his footing with each socked step slip more and more out of his control, until finally he completely lost his grip, and he skidded down the lower half of the staircase. I watched him, from the top of the landing, glaring down at him as he groaned in agony, clutching his arm.

I took a few steps down slowly to check on him, and saw his legs sprawled out on the floor, his eyes closed as he suffered from what looked more like a bruised ego than anything else. I continued to stare at him, and I let my head fall to one side to see if I could see any blood underneath him, or anything out of the ordinary surrounding him, outlining his body like chalk from the staircase to the floor.

In my elementary school cafeteria, we had an organized process for disposing of our lunches at the end of the hour. We all lined up from our bench seating, and we'd carry our trays over to the line of trash cans, each with a predetermined purpose. The first trash can was to toss out our plastic utensils. The second was meant for food and dumping out the remainder of your milk. The third was meant for the paper plate and milk carton, and finally you'd store your tray on the rack before lining up outside. This process was always the same: trash, compost, paper, tray.

On this particular day, I was thrilled to be able to sit between two of the girls in my class with whom I was closest. I had called them my friends. We walked together to the cafeteria, chatting about nothing in particular, excited that we all got to sit next to each other for forty-five minutes. After a thoroughly enjoyable lunch, we were prompted to make our way to the trash line. We stood up, and followed everyone in front of us disposing of their garbage the same way: trash, compost, paper, tray.

Making our way forward, my friend in front began to toss her plastic into the first trash bin and walked toward the compost. Reaching for my fork, I turned in time to see a small arm reach over me, haphazardly holding a carton of milk. The arm craned over my friend in the back, me, and then managed to barely make it over the first trashcan to the second. As the hand tipped over the carton, only some of the milk dribbled into the proper trash can. The majority of the chocolate milk, however, ended up in my front friend's hair, soaking her, dripping down her right pigtail.

I watched the milk drip all over the floor, and stared at the growing puddle on the ground, wondering how often lunch ladies had to clean up this type of mess, despite their methodical system that was entrusted to be upheld by children. I heard yells from adults, and looked at the woman on guard at the trash line. She began to reprimand the boy who had chosen to disrupt the system.

I stared at the boy, wondering what possessed him to try to get out of line faster than everyone else. Why did he want to skip the line, only to wait outside sooner? To go to class sooner? I couldn't understand what he was hoping to get out of this scenario. I was interrupted by my front friend's sobs, which turned to wails as people gathered around her to comfort her and call for help. I met her tear-filled eyes, and I gazed back at her, confused as to what I could do for her.

I suddenly felt so angry at the boy who'd poured the milk, but not on behalf of my friend. How could he put me in this situation? What was I supposed to do? Was I supposed to comfort her? I looked down, and noticed I was still holding the plastic fork in my right hand. I immediately dropped it into the first trash can. I stared down at my tray, only one step in the process finished. Trash, compost, paper, tray.

The sounds of sobbing started to subside as they were replaced with sniffles, words of reassurance, and yells from adults to a now snickering little boy. I poured my milk into the second trash can, and moved around the group of people, throwing my paper plate and now empty milk carton into the third trash can. I slid my tray onto the shelf, and looked back at everyone, huddled around my friend. I stood in the doorway, wondering if I should go back to her, both hands free, to show my concern for her. I started again toward her, but the lunch ladies decided to start moving the line around the commotion, and people were starting again, toward me. Trash, compost, paper, tray.

I watched as mediators moved the long-armed boy, and both of my friends off to the side to question them about what happened. I watched my dry friend explain in detail about the boy's obvious actions, while comforting my wet friend with her unforked hand, touching her arm in support. Why couldn't I have done that for my friend? Why couldn't I even look at her, or say the words I'd heard in a muted symphony around me? That it'd be okay? That I wasn't absolutely mortified to be in her presence?

I felt people bumping into me, trying to get out of the lunch room, unruffled by the last five minutes of chaos in the cafeteria. I walked through the door, thinking that not only should I have not been between my friends, but that I shouldn't have been anywhere near them. And maybe, just maybe, I could pretend I hadn't noticed what had happened. If I just told everyone I hadn't seen the mishap, I could get away with not knowing what to do, not knowing how to react. Trash, compost, paper, tray.

A loud rapping at the door startled me, and I looked toward the sound and heard a subsequent announcement of a delivery. About to run toward the door, I remembered Frank, and looked down to find an empty staircase. I slowly descended, and I opened the door to accept the food. I looked around the living room, my eyes catching the light from the kitchen.

Frank was standing at a counter, preparing the intended drinks. I set the food on the table as he walked over with a drink in each hand. He set them both down, and I began to unpack the boxes from the takeout bag. Placing items carefully in front of us, organizing them in a pattern that made sense with the placement of the drinks, the angling of the table and where we were positioned. Digging for chopsticks, I looked around the table and found no place to set them, so I handed them directly to Frank, without looking at him.

Frank began to open the container closest to him, and looked up at me.

I'm sorry you had to see that," he began.

"See what?"

Austrian Conference

I called Chloe the next day to catch up, and when she asked about Frank returning from Michigan, I gave her my version of what happened when he fell down the stairs, withholding the two hours in which I seemed to have been catatonic. I tried to make myself seem less detached, less uncaring, and tried to make the point of the story that I was proud of myself for not laughing when Frank fell. Laughing at people when they fell happened to be a nervous habit of mine since I was young that Chloe was very well aware of. Chloe—only half believing that was the intended purpose of my story—responded dully.

"Yeah, well... it's not funny when old people fall."

After chatting with my sister, I sat in silence, knowing that I had intended my phone call with Chloe to gather some insight into what had happened. My unwillingness to be completely honest with her left me empty handed, and I knew I had no one else to blame but myself. Frank had seen me essentially comatose, and I was embarrassed that I'd let my mind take over the situation in such an obvious manner.

What had my face looked like? Did he try to say anything to me? Did I say anything that I didn't remember? He had clearly known that him falling had had an effect on me, because he had apologized for doing so. But why had he done that, anyway? He had been so frantic to get downstairs, so unthinking and clumsy. And for what? Just so he could fall? I saw each of his feet, slowly losing grip on each step. How could he not have corrected himself?

I started seething, as though Frank's fall down the stairs felt like a slight, an insult. How could he put me in that position? After everything I'd been through in Michigan, I couldn't believe he had the audacity to put me through another situation like that again. Albeit, we were alone. There was no one judging silently or audibly, in my ear or from afar. I didn't have to deal with the outside assumptions, or the glares and scoffs, but I still couldn't help but feel that my presence, my continued company, made me an accomplice in something that I didn't even want to be associated with.

I imagined the woman from the hotel, so obviously repulsed by our relationship, and how I wished I could have explained to her that it wasn't exactly what it looked like, even though it was. What was happening was exactly what she thought, and she had every right to find us disgusting.

And the family? How they thought Frank had been some creep taking photos of a young woman, a stranger. The concern they showed for me, to test him, was a testament to how they perceived me, too. As better than Frank, out of his league. I couldn't get further enough away from him at that point, and the family saw that. And yet, if that's what I wanted, and it was so abundantly clear to strangers and myself, why couldn't he see it? And more importantly, why couldn't I do it?

I let my friends' feigned approval stave off my embarrassment, a temporary fix for a deeper issue. I remembered him again, falling down the stairs, and shuddered in disgust. Anger welled up inside of me, and I thought about how I'd been motionless, a shell of a person, unable to help him up, or show any sort of concern for his condition. My mind spiraled out of control with thoughts of hatred, not only of Frank, but of myself. Why couldn't I make a decision? Why do I just let things happen to me instead of taking control, of taking ownership of my actions?

I was constantly in the back seat of my own life, and this situation with Frank made me feel even more out of touch with reality. Flustered, I slid into bed in my already dark bedroom. Throwing the covers over my head, I shut my eyes tightly, wanting the world around me to disappear. Willing it not to exist, or at least to allow me to excuse myself out of it.

The world could continue to turn, and I could rejoin life when I felt ready. Reinserting myself back into life, as though I had just returned from a vacation in which I did nothing, had nothing to say, brought back no souvenirs, and had absolutely nothing to report to those around me.

Drifting off into a fitful sleep, I dreamt I was a caretaker, pushing my patient through a park. The day was pleasant, and peaceful. My companion said nothing notable, mainly pointing out the various greenery and wildlife around us. He seemed so enamored with the beauty and simplicity of the park, all the while his wheelchair became heavier and heavier, the resistance from the grass working against the large rubber wheels. I began to push him up a hill, as he pointed out the sky and the cloud formations, ignoring my pained huffs and forced kind responses to his needless comments.

I felt my resentment rising as I continued to push him up the hill, my replies to his observations fewer and further between, less and less patient, until we finally reached the peak of the hill. We stared out from the top of the mound and the beautiful sunrise, in awe of the scene before us. This time, it was I who made an observation.

"Look at the sunrise. Isn't it beautiful?"

My patient nodded in agreement, and I looked down at the back of his head, following the downward slope of the hill. Now that we'd enjoyed the sunrise, I'd have to push him down, which would be far more taxing on me than pushing him up. It'd require different muscles, a different method of movement. I'd be pulling him, not pushing him. It felt so unfair that moving down something was so easy, unless it needed to be controlled.

Lost in thought, the wheel chair slowly began to work its way down the hill. I released my hands from the handles and watched as the chair slid rapidly down the hill, bumping and catching at weird angles. The passenger didn't make a sound, submitting to the chaos, until they landed in a crumpled heap at the bottom of the hill. I did nothing, felt nothing, as I stared from above, and looked back into the horizon, wondering where I should go for my next vacation.

The next day, I found myself in a state of renewed livelihood. I knew that I couldn't possibly stay with Frank forever, but I wasn't ready to let him know that. I had to keep him thinking I was just as interested as ever, until I was ready to take control. I checked my emails to find one from Frank, having left again for Austria to give a presentation at a conference. The subject line read "in the hotel!" and I could feel his excitement radiating from my screen, and yet, felt nothing close to that myself. I read on.

"Meeting my cousins in the lobby in half an hour. I'm sweaty and need a shower. And the TV tells me a Malaysian airlines flight was shot down (probably) over Ukraine. Holy shit..."

This was my time to show concern, to keep him on the line for as long as possible.

"I read something about the Malaysian plane. Fuck, what the hell is going on in this world? Any possible update I could offer on my end seems lame in comparison to yours."

There never seemed to be any real reason to update him on the going ons of my life, because they usually garnered zero responses. I felt it was unnecessary for me to ever tell him about my daily life, as I was constantly overshadowed by him, by us. The email updates became more frequent, and I was ready to reply to each message with intention, in the ways in which each message wanted to be heard and received.

"ccc, here goes nothing...presentation in a few hours. Time to shower, head down for the included hotel breakfast and then find the University of Vienna where the conference is taking place... wish me luck! (I know you do). Full report later. Fuck, I miss you. Me"

He missed me. Okay, time to turn up the charm. I needed to be flirty, affectionate.

"Well, hey now. You're all prepared, right? You read it through to me... Once. I asked for a second time but you didn't wanna. :) You'll be fantastic. You always are. I love you dearly. Good luck!"

"God, Catherine, this email made my day for so many reasons. Yes, I think I will have a great day at the conference. Looking forward to my presentation, and getting it out-of-the-way early, and then having fun with the conference, including meeting the woman who wrote a collection about which I've written and been published. She seems to be a sweet older lady, recently retired. She wrote me a very nice letter after she read my article on her. It's a little on the warm side, but it is summer, after all. Will be good to ditch the sportcoat after the conference, and go to shorts, bathing suits, short sleeve shirts. Shit, I love you..."

I stared at his almost immediate response to my email, thinking about how easy it was for me to say things I didn't mean, and for those words to do exactly for me what I wanted them to do. Not only that, but how exhilarating it was for me to do so. I could be calculated with what I said, and how I said it. I could guide the conversations, I could finally control the narrative and what I wanted people to feel, to think of when they thought about me. I could control what I did, and what happened to me and what I did to others.

Drunk off power, my mind shifted to another question I hadn't asked myself in months: what did I want? I had been jealous of Frank's life, and that was probably why I was so infatuated with him, but how could I get there? What steps did I need to take to get away from him, but to be just like him? I thought about Frank leaving, him coming and going, his life that seemed so romantic.

I thought about when I'd started to long for him, and miss him, and realized that it was that I longed for the adventures he'd been embarking on, more than missing him. I wanted to be around a person who was doing those things because that person would somehow be a reflection of me. But people didn't see me when they saw what Frank did, they only saw him. Even when I'd gone to Michigan, it wasn't because I'd had an opportunity there, it was because he had. I'd just followed him.

If I wanted that life, if I wanted to be like him, I'd have to work hard, to study, to be diligent. If I wanted so badly to have new beginnings, new starts, I'd have to make a change.

First, I could start by leaving.

Going Rogue

For the first time in my life, I felt like I was firing on all cylinders. I started to make plans with friends, I started leaving the house, having things to say and not feeling as though every conversation had to be a rehearsal of updates and carefully planned questions to guide conversations away from myself.

My lunch dates, my discussions were impassioned, and I felt as though I was making people laugh and intriguing them in a way that I had never felt I'd been capable of before. Was this how everyone felt? Those who could openly talk with others without a looming sense of panic? How many interactions, how many friends I'd missed out on by buckling under the social pressure I'd cultivated in my own head?

Chase and I also decided to go on a few road trips during the next month, driving to Lake Tahoe first, then to Vancouver B.C. We had mutual friends in both places and were eager to visit, and take our first real road trip together. Socially and mentally, I felt up for it, too. I could feel my personality coming into fruition with my learned ability to master discussion without talking about myself.

It never had to be as controlled as I thought, because my control was focused on the person, not what I said. I needed to make people feel good about themselves when they were with me, which was far easier than what I had always tried to do, which was choose the most heavily planned responses to various outcomes. I had created a mindmap of how to encounter any and every person, not realizing that my end goal was where I should have started.

If I wanted people to like me, I'd need to make them feel good about themselves. This, as it turned out, was easy. Compliments, listening, pointed questions regarding details to said answers, people found that I was engaged, that I cared about what they had to say. These all helped me in my quest to make people feel good. In turn, this made people think highly of me.

It seemed funny to me that the trick to making people feel positively about me was to make them feel good about themselves. Really, I felt as though I myself had nothing to do with people's perceptions of me. It didn't matter who I was or what I did, because at the end of the day, the adjectives regurgitated about me would all be glowing, merely because that's how I made the other person feel. I felt calm, knowing that I could step further into society, while hiding even more of myself in plain sight.

Chase and I began our 14 hour trek down the coast to Tahoe, taking the slightly longer route so we could enjoy the coastal views. We'd stop occasionally for obligatory photos or food, laughing at everyone's doubts that we'd still remain friends after being in a car together for so long. We somehow managed to drive down to Lake Tahoe without ringing each other's necks, relieved to have reached our destination before sundown.

We were greeted by our friend and his roommate, a gorgeous woman with whom Chase immediately melted for. We'd all discussed what we'd wanted to do for our short stay in Tahoe, and decided we'd want to go to the lake the next morning, and otherwise felt indecisive about how to spend the rest of our time.

"Well," Chase started. "Let's fucking drink."

The four of us sat around the dining room table, playing drinking games and catching up. We all got chummy quickly, even the roommate with whom I was interacting with for the first time. Ultimately, we decided to play slow drinking games in an effort to break up the conversation when we needed to, while also facilitating slower, more paced drinking.

I was connecting with everyone quite well, fluidly including everyone in conversation and being able to relate and communicate at the levels in which I knew everyone wanted to be spoken to. To my friend, I regaled stories of all of my strange life updates, even humoring him and telling him I started dating a former professor of mine. He was intrigued, and supportive, with a surprising amount of acceptance and understanding. I had mainly brought it up as a sort of party story, or some kind of anecdote or ice breaker I could use in this social setting, since they wouldn't affect Frank's professional life.

I even let Chase make fun of me ruthlessly in front of everyone, all to humanize myself, to seem laid back, and able to laugh at myself. I knew that Chase had been so taken with the roommate, and thus wanted to put me down in an effort to make himself look better.

As much as I loved Chase, he was not without his shortcomings. He was deeply insecure, and was often the butt of the joke in most group settings. I'd occasionally let him use me to deter any attention toward him, mainly because I never really cared if people made fun of me, and also because I knew he'd needed people to see him in a better light than I cared to pay any mind to.

I had always been able to laugh at myself, so being self-deprecating and going along with the jabs was quite easy for me, while I also piled on to the jokes myself. Every time we changed gears, though, I noticed that Chase would try to bring the conversation back to me, which, with every obvious attempt, started to make everyone else feel uncomfortable. I felt stuck between wanting to help Chase feel more secure and confident, while also trying to appease the other two people in the room who clearly lost interest and started to feel the topic was getting a little too aggressive.

Instead of getting in my head or overthinking, I simply went with the masses, and decided to ask everyone else what they'd been up to, ignoring Chase's affronts. First, I listened as our friend told us about his fiancé, and how happy he was to be with her. He proudly showed us a photo, her sporting a massive sunburn, but also chiseled abs.

"Aw, she's cute! And dude, she's ripped!" I said.

I felt compelled to validate her, and though everything I said was true, I surprised myself by my compliment, specifically by how naturally it came and the lack of effort at the statement. Chase started, and we all began to tense as we considered how he'd try to drunkenly bring me down again.

"My girlfriend is... she's really big."

Chase slowly pulled out his phone to show us a photo of them together, and she nearly doubled him in girth. I had been surprised, not because there was anything particularly wrong with her size, but because he had never mentioned it to me before.

Had I not been as close to Chase as I thought I'd been? Did he only bring this up because he saw how fit our friend's fiancé was, and he felt as though he needed to admit a secret? Or perhaps, did he feel bad about putting me down for so long, and he saw my actions and how I was unfazed and being kind, and he felt the need to somehow make up for putting me down and found talking about their significant others' bodies would be a good way to elbow into the conversation?

I was doing it again. I shook my head to get out of it.

"Is she actually that big?"

Our friend directed the question at me, and I glanced over at Chase before admitting that I'd never actually met her in person.

"But you guys are best friends! How have you never met his girlfriend?"

Chase looked mortified, and I sympathetically made eye contact before responding earnestly that she had no interest in meeting me, so it just never happened.

"Well, that's probably for the best. She'd probably freak out if she saw how much better looking you are than her."

I laughed in shock, and Chase kept his gaze cast downward. Chase didn't dare respond or look up, and it dawned on me that perhaps, it was never his girlfriend that didn't want to meet me, but that it had been through Chase's calculated and intentional efforts that I was never able to meet any of his girlfriends.

We all decided to change the subject, and I focused on talking to the roommate, getting to know her a little better and complimenting her to establish a sense of camaraderie. I always felt as though I never did a good enough job connecting to people, and thus intended to make her feel as included as possible, inviting her into our inside jokes and asking about her life.

She seemed relaxed, completely uneager to try to impress, which made me like and respect her in a way that made us fast friends. My new-found ability to connect with people quickly bound me to her, and our friend began to gravitate more toward us as well, further excluding Chase from the group.

Chase became aware of the drift and attempted to make more insulting comments at me. I swerved and shrugged them off. My cavalier reactions infuriated him more, and even though I could tell he was coming from a place of hurt, and wanting to feel included, I didn't feel like accepting his hurled insults to bolster his ego. I let him flounder, pretended not to notice his suffering, all while knowing I could essentially blame my negligence on the alcohol.

The games had fallen to the wayside during our discussions and jokes, so we had decided to pick it back up again. Chase found this the proper opportunity to talk smack, bringing up Frank at any opportunity. Mid-eye roll, I heard the roommate call out Chase in my defense.

"Shut up, you little nancy."

My eyes, unable to complete a full circle, shot to Chase instantly. One of the reasons Chase had always deferred to his hyper-masculine coworkers and submitted to their whims was because he was transparently insecure about his masculinity. He had never necessarily confided this in me, and I hadn't even been sure that he was aware of it, but whenever the topic of him somehow being less than manly came into question, Chase felt threatened. I knew he would be wounded, especially, because a beautiful woman had called him a feminine pejorative.

I stared, quietly, with my mouth completely agape. At no point did Chase look at me, but shot daggers at the roommate, who had no idea the damage she had caused by that comment.

"Oh, really? Is that what you think?" Chase sneered, slurring his speech slightly.

He proceeded to grab the half-drunk bottle of vodka from the middle of the table, hastily unscrewing the top and pouring a sloppy shot into the tiny glass in front of him. Wildly, he brought the shot to his lips, threw it back, and slammed it on the table. He continued to do this three more times, before I decided to put an end to his misguided display.

"Chase, I think that's enough," I started.

"Oh! You think it's enough?" Chase's lips curled as he glared at me, resenting that he had been the butt of the evening's joke, despite his greatest efforts to crown me the jester.

Torn, I stared back at my friend. Couldn't I have just taken the heat for one night? To be fair, I was perfectly willing to try, but he was doing far too well making himself look idiotic. It wasn't my responsibility to try to make him look good, especially because he was doing such a great job of painting himself a fool.

We continued our games, Chase ostracizing himself more and more by angrily excusing himself to smoke cigarettes outside, despite the chill. Slamming doors, and aggressively scraping his chair legs as he stomped in and out of the house, we all exchanged raised eyes and chuckled. Eventually, Chase barked that he'd be going to the corner store to get more cigarettes.

"You can't," our friend replied. "The store is definitely closed."

"Oh, I can't?" Spittle began to form in the corners of Chase's mouth. I couldn't look away.

"Also, there are little bears out here. Look."

The roommate brought out her phone, showing us a video from a few days prior of a bear digging through the neighbor's trash can in the middle of the day.

"I was about to leave for work when I saw this. I couldn't believe it!"

"Oh, there are bears here?"

Chase's attempts at witty counters became just repeating what people said in a sarcastic manner, which I began to find incredibly entertaining. At everyone's pleas and behest, Chase only felt more emboldened to leave, willing to brave whatever would come his way on his quest for cigarettes. He stormed out, all of us unable to convince him otherwise, and us too drunk to try too much harder than we already had.

An hour passed, and caught up in our conversations, we had almost forgotten about Chase until we heard the front door slam. Startled, our heads jerked in unison toward the living room, me leaning slightly backwards in my chair to angle my head to see who had walked in. In a huff, Chase charged back into the dining room.

"The fucking store was closed," Chase yelled.

"Yeah man, that's what I tried to tell you about a hundred times," my friend shot back.

"Well, you should have tried harder to stop me, then."

"Dude, we all tried. Don't be ridiculous. You couldn't be reasoned with."

"Well, I'm sure if I was a girl or something, people would have tried a lot harder to keep me from wandering around outside by myself."

Chase's logic seemed unsound as he changed angles. For some reason, this bothered me in my drunken stupor, and I decided to call him out on it.

"I thought this whole posturing thing you were doing was because you didn't want to be treated as a female? That's what you wanted. So, we just let you make your own decisions like the big man you are."

The last four words of my insult slipped out like venom, seeping into his vodka-soaked brain. Our friend and the roommate laughed, and began chatting again, not realizing the depths at which my words truly stung Chase. I maintained eye contact with him, curious to see what types of things he'd throw my way. He had spent all night chiding me, every carelessly thrown dart missing me by miles, while my one calculated arrow sunk deep into him, burning a hole in his chest. The anger dissipated from Chase's eyes as they began to well up with tears.

For a moment, I started to feel guilty for what I'd done. Hadn't I let Chase poke fun because I knew I could handle it? Why did I feel the need to let him sink even lower, always the lesser of in a group of any size?

I stifled my thoughts, wondering why I had even bothered to pity him. If Chase had been willing to make me out to be the easy target, then I couldn't waste any more effort trying to be more embarrassing than him. Chase was a threat unto himself, and I knew there was nothing to be done but to watch him crumble under his own efforts.

Luckily for him, no one else had noticed his tears as he quietly excused himself to the bathroom.

Another hour passed, and our excited exchanges were interrupted by my own need to utilize the restroom. We had all then remembered that Chase was still occupying the facilities, and as I was heading there anyway, I had assured everyone I'd check on him.

I knocked on the door, and after not hearing any response, I called out to him.

"Chase?" I was greeted with silence.

I wiggled the doorknob, which was unlocked.

"Okay," I warned. "I'm coming in to check on you..."

I opened the door, uncertain but infinitely curious as to what I'd find. My eyes dropped to the area behind the door to find Chase seated, pants down, shirt pulled up to his nipples on the toilet. A smile spread deviously across my face, so in awe with the set up. I couldn't get enough of Chase, finding him in such a vulnerable state. I had so many questions.

Why had he decided to bring his shirt up so high onto his torso? How long had he been asleep? At any point, had he been fully crying, or did it stop at just the tears? The bathroom was suddenly a feast for my eyes. I couldn't get enough of my good fortune, and I let myself giggle. I'd even wondered if he had been taking a shit, or if he just decided to sit down to rest. Remembering that I had to pee urgently, I reluctantly decided to end my enjoyment.

"Uh... Chase." I lifted a finger to tap him, unsure of which part of his body would be least invasive to touch.

In my liquor-addled state, I looked at the excessively exposed skin, tracing his body from afar, one eye open to help me focus on where I should poke him. Ultimately, I tapped the top of his head, which jolted him awake.

"Oh." He rested his elbow on his upper thigh, and let his chin slump heavily into his palm. "Hi."

"I, uh. I need to use the bathroom. Can you hurry up in here?"

"Sure, give me a second." He had made no attempt to cover up, submitting to the manner in which I'd found him.

I nodded, and as though someone had pressed a rewind button on me, I moved out of the bathroom by twirling gracefully in the opposite direction from which I walked in, and closed the door behind me.

From the dining room, I could hear murmurs asking how Chase had been doing. Drunk on Grey Goose and intoxicated by the scene I'd just witnessed, I let myself burst out laughing. I walked slowly back into the dining room, tears streaming down my face from my feeble attempts to suppress my laughter.

I gave myself time to breathe as my friends waited eagerly for my report. For a moment, I thought that perhaps I should have kept it to myself. Hadn't Chase had enough humiliation for the evening? Did I need to describe in detail his position, his peculiar choice in undressing? Part of me wanted to help my friend maintain some of his dignity from the evening, but the realization slowly crept over me between cackles and gasps for air that he had, essentially, been that exposed for the entire evening.

All along, he had been the roast at the feast. Us teasing him, sampling the goodness he was providing us in his attempts to be cool, to fit in, this had been provided for us, courtesy of Chase. Yes, my friends deserved to know. He had been there for us all night, just as he was in the bathroom where I found him.

He had been flayed, his legs spread out wide for us to rip off, his skin crispy from the ridicule. He had been on a platter for us to feed upon all night, I was simply cutting slices for my friends and serving them their main course.

Miles To Go

I had awoken on the couch in the living room the next morning, and saw Chase on the floor beneath me. I heard creaking from the top of the staircase and watched our friend descend. He groaned lazily and yawned, rubbing his eyes and motioned his chin in greeting, mouth wide, before making his way to the bathroom.

I reached over Chase toward the table to grab my phone to check the time, when I remembered I should probably check for updates from Frank. Half-heartedly scrolling through emails, I found one with a stylistically familiar trailing email subject: "you, me..."

I tapped the subject to open. "California?"

It occurred to me that I hadn't even told Frank I'd be in Lake Tahoe, so I thought it a fun opportunity to do so now. I positioned my body flat on the couch, and aimed my phone upwards so that I could take a photo of myself with Chase passed out beneath me.

Laughing, I typed out "Well, what do you know?" in the subject line, attaching the photo in the body and finishing off with "we're here now. Or, more like, on the Nevada side of Tahoe.

Close enough, though. See you tomorrow?" I joked, knowing Frank was still very much traipsing through Europe.

I thought about what California would entail, though. Frank would be going straight from Europe to California, wrapping up his chaotic summer by visiting his old hometown before settling into the school year routine. Me, go there? I'd been to California many times before, and although not opposed to any of those visits, the idea of going with Frank seemed superfluous.

I had followed him to Michigan for the newness, the adventure of not having been there before, yet the idea of going somewhere I'd frequented left me feeling far more vulnerable than going somewhere completely uncharted. It wasn't so much that the idea or memory of California would somehow be tainted with Frank there, but more that I wouldn't know how to act with him in a comfortable setting that we'd never existed in before together.

At school, no matter what capacity our relationship had been, we knew how to operate together. In his home, it was the same feeling. In an unexplored place, we could truly be whoever and whatever we wanted to be to each other. Somewhere known to each of us in different capacities seemed much trickier, a collision of our past experiences forcing us to maneuver around the shrapnel with precision and care.

My frequent vacations to Disneyland in my youth, my family who lived near the beach in Los Angeles, my childhood friend Darla who'd moved to San Diego a few years after high school. For Frank, though, it was his home. He had grown up there, spent his childhood there...

It suddenly dawned on me that this trip to California Frank had just invited me on may have been for fun, but chances were, he was wanting me to meet his parents. We had really only been together for a few months, but could he feel ready to actually introduce me to his mother and father?

Not wanting to get ahead of myself, I closed my eyes and focused on today's activities. I'd be going to the lake with my friends. I'd be actively avoiding speaking of the previous night's details in front of Chase, not wanting to provoke or dredge anything that would rile him up further. Today would be a fun day with friends, carefree, and there was no reason to assume anyone expected anything from me.

My friend exited the bathroom and strode directly toward me, grabbing my legs and bunching them toward my torso, collapsing them like an accordion. I laughed and moved my knees closer to my chest. He threw his legs up onto the table, and peered down at Chase on the ground.

"Have you guys spoken at all?"

"No fucking way. He stirred a bit, but I'm not sure which angle to play. Do I make fun of him, or pretend that nothing happened?"

My friend considered, then responded that we should all pretend as though nothing happened, otherwise we'd have another replay today.

"But, let's kick him awake now for fun."

We slowly moved our feet on top of Chase's lifeless body, gingerly resting them on his side facing upright. I placed my left foot on his shoulder, my right on his ribs. My friend carefully placed his feet on Chase's hip and upper thigh. We made dramatic eye contact, nodded, and began to tap dance all over Chase.

Chase groaned as my friend and I laughed, us moving our legs up and down the length of his side. Chase started to laugh too, feeling perhaps that all had been forgiven from the night before, happy to be included in the group. Knowing that the roommate would be at work today, I knew that Chase would have an immense amount of pressure taken off of him to be cool or seem tough, and that we could all suffer in silence of our hangovers together, and move past the transgressions of last night.

"Now turn over," I taunted. "We have to even out the massage on the other side."

We got ready quickly, all of us agreeing not to eat breakfast or need any food to look swimsuit skinny for the lake. I kicked back onto the couch, waiting for everyone else to finish up, and I pulled out my phone again. Finding another vague-subjected message, I rapidly opened the email.

"Catherine, Catherine...

Looks like you and Chase had fun last night. What'd you get up to?

Didn't realize you'd be gone, away, but I'm glad you are having a good time.

So, if you're free next week, I figure we can explore Southern California together. And, if you're up for it, I figured you could meet my parents..."

"Hey, Cat, let's load up the car."

Without taking my eyes off my phone, I felt around for the bags we'd packed with towels, snacks, other beachy items, slung them over my shoulders, and walked knowingly out the front door.

I hated that I had been right about Frank wanting me to meet his parents, mainly because I had quelled that suspicion in an effort not to get ahead of myself. I didn't want to be right when I overthought things, yet it seemed to always serve me well to continue to do so. Was I ready to meet Frank's parents? I had known that I had every intention of leaving him, that I couldn't possibly be happy with him for any much longer.

I had once broken up with an ex, and despite his pleas to get me to stay, I resisted and forcefully stood my ground.

"What if we just continued having sex?" He had suggested.

"I really don't think that's a good idea..." I started.

"Hear me out. That way, you can still have orgasms and I can still spend time with you."

This arrangement sounded quite pathetic, but I agreed, knowing that it would be a bad idea. I acquiesced because really, if that's what he said he was okay with, why was it my responsibility to foresee that it wouldn't be? Certainly, the sex had always been good, but I was slowly getting irritated with him, growing tired of him, losing respect for him as a person.

It reached a breaking point eventually, and I drove over to his house one last time, knowing that I would be sleeping with him, and ending the compromise promptly afterwards. The sinking feeling in my stomach as I drove over suggested that I knew what I was doing was wrong, but I rationalized it to myself.

I told myself that I don't socialize often, and I wouldn't know when I'd be having sex again, so I may as well just do this one last time before an indefinite dry spell.

I pulled up to his apartment, we barely spoke as he let me in, and I walked past him up the stairs to his bedroom, waiting for him to trail behind me. I had already started to take my clothes off before he reached his bedroom, and promptly following suit, he closed the door and I laid down on his bed. He had crawled toward me, burying his face between my legs, and I closed my eyes and moaned unencumbered until it was over.

I decided that excusing myself to the restroom would be the perfect opportunity to get dressed and check in on myself. I entered the bathroom, and stared at myself in the mirror. My hair was tousled in a way that suggested I'd been at the beach all day, lived in yet manageable. Part of me wished I had been wearing an uglier shirt, or that I looked less attractive, so as to cushion the blow of what I was about to do. I ran my fingers through my hair, thinking that I could catch a snag, a tangle, and bring it to the forefront so he could fixate on a flaw of some kind.

How inconvenient that my face and body seemed riddled with flaws at most points in time, aside from when I needed them most. I had wanted to make him feel better, by making me look worse, yet I couldn't find a single thing wrong with me to make this better for him. Defeated, I headed back to the bedroom, relieved to find that he'd gotten dressed, and was sitting on the bed, waiting for me.

"Thank fucking god." I thought. "I really didn't want to have to break up with him naked."

I sat down next to him on the bed, and he looked up at me, sadness and expectation in his eyes.

"Hey, I think we need to stop doing this. I knew it'd be a bad idea from the start, and I realize how selfish it is for me to keep stringing you along like this. I need to put my foot down. It isn't fair to you. I'm sorry."

I hugged him from the side, and stood up, grabbing my long sweater I'd tactfully brought to stuff any of my leftover belongings from his place, bundling everything up in my arms.

His eyes welled up with tears.

"Wait, did you know you were going to break up with me before you got here?"

Stunned, caught, seen, I paused in disbelief.

"Well, no, I... I didn't. I didn't know. I mean, I'd been thinking about it, and I just."

I stammered and stuttered. I couldn't believe he had actually called me out.

"So, you came here, knowing you were going to leave me, and you fuck me? You fucked me and you knew you were going to end things with me? How could you do that? I'm a goddamn person, Catherine!"

I knew I couldn't lie or talk my way out of the mess I'd created, so I took one more sweeping look around the room and walked out.

"How could you?"

He followed me down the stairs, begging for answers I was unwilling to give him.

"Okay, so if you didn't know before you arrived, then, when did you decide? Was it before or after you came? Before or after I pulled my ejaculating dick out of you?"

I cringed at how vulgar he was being, knowing he was talking out of anger. I knew that the only way for me to win the verbal joust was to tell him the truth. I hated that he had been right, and I couldn't let him know how right about me he'd been.

I walked out the front door, gliding faster and faster to my car. He ran in front of me, and as I threw my things into the backseat, he grabbed my shoulders.

"Don't touch me."

He lifted his hands and kept them up, as though my sense of touch might not have been able to register the lack of pressure before my eyes saw his unobstructed hands.

"Okay, no problem. But Catherine, I love you."

I stared at him, confused by his Hail Mary. Had he expected me to say it back? Clearly, if I had broken up with him before, and was now ending only the physical part of the relationship, my feelings for him were essentially nonexistent. But what if I did say I loved him back? I'd wondered what that'd imply, if I threw those words in, despite all my actions screaming otherwise.

"I love you, too," I answered lazily.

His eyes lit up, and he began to start into his argument.

"It's just..." I interrupted him. "Not that much."

I watched his jaw drop, and I used his shock to make my escape. I opened my car door, bumping him out of the way. I slammed the door and drove off, watching him get smaller and smaller from my rearview mirror, staring at me in horror.

We arrived at Lake Tahoe, and we all laid out our towels and set up our area. I laid back on my towel, and remembered I hadn't replied to Frank. I thought about how I could visit Darla, maybe even have Frank meet her so she and I could talk about what on earth had been going on in my head. It might be interesting, yes, to see how Frank would fare in an element out of his comfort zone, needing to fit in with someone from my life, instead of me needing to meld into his. Then, I could meet his parents, charm them, and make them think highly of me.

I propped myself up on my forearms, and ran my fingers through my wind-teased hair.

"Sure, I'll visit Darla and then I'll see you there. Details later."

Almost as soon as I'd replied, I'd received a response.

"Holy shit. Really? I'll let them know. Oh, CCC... I'm excited. They'll love you. I love you..."

"I love you, too." I typed.

Just not that much.

Meet the Friend

With Darla as accommodating as ever, by the next week I was already back south visiting my old friend. Darla and I had been friends since junior high school, and although we hadn't lived in close proximity to each other since then, we'd always been able to fall back into comfort without ever trying too hard.

Her willingness to make arrangements coupled with her quiet confidence made her incredibly generous and agreeable to be around. She never tried too hard to impress anyone, and was often in her own world, always seemingly unaffected. I'd always made fun of her for reacting immediately, giving the blasé "cool" or "yeah…" types of answers, showing zero indication that she had processed or understood a single word I'd said.

I'd joked that her famous last words would be "yeah… wait, what?" And yet, she was always reliable, deep, and willing to go above and beyond without actually exerting much effort.

Her impeccable timing enabled her to scoop me up from arrivals and peel off, us falling back into our relationship without skipping a beat. As I expected, the prying commenced.

"Okay, so, explain this to me again?"

She tried to steal a few glances from the road at me while tucking her long black hair behind her ear.

"I mean, it's pretty straight forward…" I teased. "I'm in a relationship with this guy who used to be my professor."

The delay in Darla's reaction caught me off guard, the seconds feeling like hours. It assured me, however, that she was in fact listening, and processing.

"Well," she considered, finally cutting through the silence, "just. Oh my god, okay, and he's going to come get you from my place? So, I'll get to meet him?"

My mind buzzed, thinking about how funny it'd be to see a grown man, sitting in a three-bedroom apartment in San Diego with two young women half his age. How out of place would he feel in housing fit for university students?

I couldn't wait for Darla to actually meet him, then, so we could text about him on the drive to visit his parents. I thought about how much pleasure I'd get from seeing how everyone would interact in the scenario, reveling in the awkwardness. I looked over at Darla who seemed to be lost in thought, a smile slowly spreading across her face.

"This'll be fun," she said.

Our few days together flew by as Darla would go to work in the mornings and arrive back at her apartment before I even considered getting out of bed. I felt as though she were constantly on the go. I was rubbing my eyes as she popped into the room, springy and bouncy as she put her jacket back into her closet.

"I don't know how you do it," I moaned.

"I'm honestly good with just a little bit of sleep," Darla shrugged. "I can get through."

I shook my head and grabbed my phone, knowing I'd be receiving some kind of correspondence from Frank.

"CCC... Address? I'm on my way. See you in two hours."

Panicked, I gasped and looked up at Darla.

"Dude, he's coming now. He's already on his way."

Darla's eyes widened, and she let out a little chuckle.

"When did he send that message?"

It didn't even dawn on me to check how much time had been eaten away from my two hour window, and I let out a meek sigh of relief and slumped back in bed, seeing it was only sent half an hour ago.

"I've got about an hour and a half of freedom," I spat dramatically, staring at the ceiling.

"Well, better get your ass out of bed and pack."

As quickly as I'd shot out of bed, I was ready, which made waiting around for Frank that much more grueling. I paced back and forth in Darla's living room, her eyes following my every step with great amusement.

"Hear me out. Why don't you just sit down and chill? I'll put something on the TV."

I reluctantly sat down, and almost as soon as I began to relax, my phone rang.

My heart sank and I gave Darla a look, which she met with the same anxious expression. I stood up, and answered after a long sigh.

"Hello? I'm walking outside to meet you."

I hastened to find him as the burning in my chest moved its way to my stomach. Walking out of the parking lot, I had to remind myself that I might not immediately recognize him. Every time I saw him, every time he left and came back, he resembled another person to me, someone almost familiar, but someone I never really knew.

Exiting the mouth of the parking lot, I turned my gaze up the hill to find a tall, lumbering man walking toward me. He stopped when he saw me, smiled, and resumed his march, faster, his legs bordering on buckling as he made his way down the hill toward me. He stopped for a moment in front of me, and then brought me into an embrace. I let my face absorb fully into his torso, making no attempt to move my head to either side.

For some reason, this idea amused me, and I managed to edge out a muffled greeting directly into his stomach. Frank released me, and I gazed up at him, wondering if I should try to look more pleased to see him. Were my arms even around him when he hugged me? I looked back toward the apartment, and thought about how awkward Darla and Frank's meeting would be, and my eyes sparkled with yearning.

"Hey..." I said lazily, "Come inside. My friend is excited to meet you."

I walked ahead of him, my pace intended to give Darla a little bit of a warning before welcoming a stranger into her home. As an added bonus, I didn't tell Darla a single thing about Frank, nothing about his age or appearance, and I wanted to see her take everything in at once.

I opened the door, and Darla perked up from the couch. I gave her a wink, and ushered Frank into the room. I sat down across from Darla on the couch, letting Frank stand in the doorway to introduce himself. I wanted nothing but to witness the introduction, to merely allow Frank into Darla's life and to let them see how they'd interact with each other, how they'd handle it. I looked coolly up at Frank, and then fixed my eyes on Darla.

Her face remained composed, although she let her eyes dart subtly between Frank and I. Frank continued to stand in the door dumbly, looking between me and Darla waiting for me to formally introduce him. Darla started to chuckle, and rolling her eyes at me, she looked at Frank and introduced herself.

"Also," she added, "you can sit down."

I laughed silently and inched over, slapping the previously occupied area next to me. Frank waved, and introduced himself as well, a bit shaken by the den he'd walked into.

"So, what do you guys have planned?"

Frank looked at me inquisitively, and I stared back, waiting for him to answer Darla's innocent question.

"Well…" Frank started, "I think we're going to go to Disneyland, maybe."

He continued to shoot me sideways glances. My eyes never left him as I watched him flounder, taking it all in as he was fidgeting and far more distressed than I could have ever imagined he would be.

"But that's if it's sunny, of course… but if it's, well…"

What the fuck was this? It took every fiber of my being to suppress my laughter and contain my enjoyment.

"But I heard it might be raining one of those days, and so we might have to just do something indoors, but honestly, it's hard to know… to plan for…"

I watched his body, his face, his hands moving spastically, my eyes tracing his body, his outline looking more and more transplanted by the second. He looked crudely photoshopped into life, into a world of 22 year olds who were in on a secret that he would only ever be a part of by being the butt of the joke.

"And, well, so despite the weather, I think Catherine and I are going to have dinner with my parents."

I took this moment to steal a glance from Darla, who happened to look at me at the same time. She glanced back at Frank, her eyes wide, but kind, and she nodded as though she were impressed with him.

"Wow. Sounds like you've got it all figured out. That is, unless the weather doesn't cooperate. Then you're fucked."

I tore my eyes away from Darla to stare back at Frank, whose jaw dropped slightly. I decided to laugh to ease the tension, which allowed Darla a way to fall out of the conversation and let myself in. Frank swallowed hard and looked at me.

"Shall we?"

I nodded and pushed myself up toward Darla, giving her a full hug and thanking her for her hospitality. I grabbed my bag and set off toward the door, my eyes set to leave, my ears waiting to hear the farewell between Darla and Frank.

"It was very nice to meet you." Frank said politely.

"Yeah, same to you." Darla responded, adding "be careful out there!"

As soon as the door closed behind us, I set off walking in front of Frank, grabbing my phone to text Darla, but before I could unlock my phone, a message appeared.

"Oh my god. What the fuck. Hahaha. He's so old, dude"

Darla was a step ahead of me, ready to drag Frank to filth.

Hungrily, I responded, "That was amazing. He was so nervous, he had no idea what to do."

"And why was he so obsessed with the weather?" Darla chirped back.

"Right? God, he really found his theme. I felt like I was watching someone audition for a part, without a fucking clue what was on the green screen behind them."

"Well, have fun with that. Weather that storm, girl."

Still staring and laughing at my phone, I walked up to the passenger side of the car, waiting to hear the click to indicate it was unlocked. After a strange amount of time, I noticed the door hadn't been unlocked, and I looked across the top of the car at Frank, who had been staring at me.

"What's so funny?" he urged.

"Oh, nothing. I'm just texting my friend."

Frank continued to glare at me, so I let a weak, warm smile spread across my face.

"Are you okay?" I asked, innocently.

He committed to the staring match for a minute, before relenting and unlocking the door.

We finally sat down, and as I started to buckle myself in, I thanked Frank for opening the door.

"Thank goodness you finally unlocked the car. I thought I was starting to feel rain."

The Weather Man's Home

For the entirety of the drive from San Diego to Long Beach, Frank and I didn't speak a word to each other. The silence was filled with his occasional throat clearings from the driver's seat and me singing and humming along to songs on the radio, gazing dreamily outside at the view.

There was a small part of me that wanted to apologize to Frank, just to smooth things over. However, there lived a much larger part of me that wanted him to broach the subject, if he saw fit, and to pretend I hadn't noticed and welcomed the way Darla and I had treated him so that I could gaslight him and make him feel like it was all in his head.

There existed an even smaller, albeit still present part of me that wanted to bring it up myself, to ask him what he thought about it, to taunt him and rub it in his face once more. However, the part of me that won out was the part that couldn't care less about Frank, and would rather hum along to myself and watch the colors in strokes pass me by.

I had dozed off during the tail end of our ride, and woke up to Frank's gentle voice.

"Hey Rin, we're here."

I opened my eyes ever so slightly to see the two story, suburban, upper-middle class home in front of me. Completely unimpressed, I gave him a light smile and reached around to grab my bag from the backseat.

Frank's face moved closer to mine, thinking I was leaning in to give him a kiss, and my fist narrowly missed his face in my attempt to retrieve my belongings. He paused, his face an inch from my cheek, and we both stopped and looked at each other, from an awkwardly close distance.

"Oh, you thought I was…"

"Yeah, sorry. I just thought you were leaning in to kiss me." Frank interrupted, sounding suspiciously heartened by his error.

He continued to stare at me expectantly, as though his veiled apology was actually a request. I glanced away from him to search for my bag. I grabbed my belongings, and my eyes met his once more. They hadn't let up their anticipation, their hope for a kiss, and I found myself staring at his lips.

They were the same color as the skin of his face, which I found odd because I didn't quite know where his lips ended and where the rest of his face began. My eyes darted back and forth between his eyes and where I believed his lips to be, and I decided that, since I couldn't tell where his actual lips were, that I'd kiss him on the cheek.

I gave him a quick peck and smiled at my strained logic, where Frank, thinking I'd smiled out of flirtation, beamed brightly at me, the skin around the gaping hole in his face stretching from ear to ear.

We both exited the car in unison, and I stood in front of the garage door, waiting for him to put in the code to open it. I scanned the house, and peered down the street at the individual dwellings. Each home was a duplicate of its neighbor, cookie cutter versions of itself multiplying and spreading like a virus. How hard is it to keep up with the Joneses? Each of these houses must have cost the exact same amount, depending on inflation and gentrification.

"Let's go inside," Frank bellowed out to me, and I took one last glance down the street of monotony and entered one of the carbon copies.

The interior, although with far more zhuzh and personality than the exterior, still felt lacking. Frank showed me around, pointing out each room and the functions they so obviously served. Here's the kitchen, where we do kitchen things. Here's the bathroom, where we do bathroom things. Here's the living room, where we live. With each room we entered, Frank would turn around to look at me, to drink in my expression. I looked around politely, nodding back at him in reassurance, wondering what it was he wanted from me.

Not that he needed to make any attempt to impress me, but I was confused as to what it was that I was supposed to be saying or doing. And more importantly, why did it matter? This was his childhood home, not mine, and however special or significant it was to him was what mattered, certainly not what I thought about it.

He led me up the stairs, hyper aware of his pace and each step he took. I watched each of his feet finding the right step as he glanced down after every few to ensure he hadn't lost his footing. As we rounded the corner at the top of the stairs,

Frank stopped suddenly to introduce yet another room. The slight moment of pause followed promptly by a sharp inhale and sigh indicated he'd be presenting me something he felt was very dramatic and meaningful.

"And this is my bedroom." The voice in my head and Frank said this in unison.

Frank's childhood bedroom was small, with light blue accents, a similar color palate to his current, adult bedroom. My eyes scanned the room, taking it in, and I gave him another gentle smirk in encouragement.

"Looks familiar..." I joked.

"You don't say?" Frank jeered back. "I guess old habits die hard."

"Doesn't mean they shouldn't die, though," I thought to myself.

Frank looked at me curiously. "What, you don't like my room? Either of them?"

I blinked rapidly, realizing that I had actually spoken those thoughts out loud. I let my coy smile spread a bit farther, hoping to smooth over my oversight.

"Only trying to get a rise out of you," I chirped, and walked deeper into the room, trying to be more intent about analyzing his bedroom. There were family photos, a signed baseball... all of the items that would have seemed carefully planted for an open house.

"Okay, so you were into baseball." I tried to continue to ask him questions that I didn't really care about, to further myself from the rude slip of the tongue moments ago.

"Yeah, I started playing when I was about 4 years old..."

Frank began explaining his interest in baseball, why he wanted to start playing, all while I tuned him out and resumed perusing his childhood. I walked toward the window, and looked down at the view. The backyard was sizable, even with the full-sized pool. I thought about how insignificant that pool must have been to everyone in that family, and in that neighborhood.

I peered over the fence at the neighbor, who'd had the exact same layout and set up of a backyard. It seemed like something that was so compulsory that it was often taken for granted. How could it be special if everyone in the cul-de-sac had it? I supposed Frank had had some cousins from the Midwest who would come and visit, and I guessed that they would have been in awe of the pool, always included on the tour of the house.

"Wow!" I'd imagine a little kid saying. "I can't believe it! A pool! At your own house!"

A young, baseball hat wearing Frank, shrugged, cocked his head and raised his hands.

"Oh, it's nothing!" waving it away dismissively, while sporting a proud grin.

Frank came up from behind me and hugged me, his arms around my shoulders. Instinctively, I brought my hands up to his, squeezing him closer.

"So, now you've seen how I've grown up! What do you think? Does it all make sense now?"

I considered how much you could gather from an adult based on their childhood bedroom. What would Frank have thought about my childhood bedroom? Even if it had still been around, I would have never invited him in. I'd always despised when people would enter my bedroom. I'd gasp when someone came into my room, startled by the gall, feeling too unprepared, too vulnerable, too exposed. Toys and Pokemon cards mutated to clothes and random sheets of paper as I got older, littering the carpet.

The only bit of respite from the chaos was a path I'd cleared from the door to my bed. I'd thought about the weird cup of scabs I'd had as a collection, always finding my own and other people's fascinating. I'd even had two journals.

One was fake, naturally, to thwart the prying eyes of my parents. That journal was reserved for the boring monotony of adolescence, like going to class or having a crush on a boy, maybe throwing in the occasional spicy detail to ensure my parents actually bought that it was a legitimate journal. The real journal, however, I'd kept strategically hidden in my dresser. I'd pull out each drawer ever so slightly, so that the journal could slip behind the back of the moveable drawer and into the space between the actual drawers and the backing of the dresser. Retrieving the journal was always an incredible hassle, but there was always a sense of accomplishment and excitement when I would pull it out.

If my parents had been listening at the door, or curious about why I was constantly opening and closing so many drawers, I knew their search to find hidden goods was futile. They'd never find the true book of revelations, in which I'd detail cheating on tests, worrying about getting pregnant, and how I'd been getting rides home from my lacrosse coach, who took my virginity when I was 14. Or that I'd cheated on that lacrosse coach with one of the boys on the team that had a crush on me.

That room presented itself as lawless, sheer pandemonium, yet harbored a carefully guarded, meticulous secret. A secret which was masked by the disorder, taking up the smallest amount of space. It snickered, an inside joke in the corner, drowned out by the yells and shouts from the carelessness scattered across the floor. I felt like a magician, distracting a captive audience with one hand, all while slighting them with the other.

I loosened my grip on Frank's arms, causing him to release his embrace. I scanned the room again, taking him in with fresh eyes, compared his room to mine. His was tidy, honest. Everything that represented him was presented proudly. This was the room of someone with nothing to hide, someone that greeted newcomers, someone who wanted to be understood and loved and accepted. Certainly, his room did make sense now. He made sense now.

"Ready to meet my parents for dinner? We're going to meet them at this diner down the road."

"Oh, we aren't eating here?"

Had we really just come to his house so he could give me a tour? Truly, meeting Frank's parents after us only being together for a couple of months, and him showing me his childhood home, he was invested in this. He was invested in us. Far more than I was, and far more than I'd ever intended to be.

His embrace in his bedroom suddenly held more meaning, as though he were testing out what our future would be like, gazing upon our yard, envisioning children running and screaming by the pool...

Making our way outside, I took one last glance at the American Dream. Driving off to dinner, I watched the identical houses whizz by me, the white and nude color combinations whirling and streaking together.

I closed my eyes, the colors and strokes of mundanity too painful to see, like a record skipping over and over before my eyes. Even with my eyes closed, the streaks and lines were burned into my memory, like white picket fences guarding this world from me. This life that was so alien, such a stranger to me.

This life that I had never been a part of.

This life that I knew I never would be a part of.

Meet the Parents

A few days later I found myself in bed, on my stomach, propped up on my forearms like a sphynx. In front of me was my open laptop, my right fingertips gliding over the keyboard, my left hand occupied with my credit card. My index finger danced in circles around the mouse pad, second guessing my decision to click "Confirm Payment".

Frank and I had driven off to the diner at the end of his street to meet up with his parents. We parked in front of the picture windows, and Frank ducked his head to see inside a bit clearer, avoiding the glare. At that moment, a man and woman in their late sixties turned around to gaze back at us, waving animatedly. I imagined they were in a commercial for a cruise line, beckoning us to join in on their adventure.

Walking in, the bell chimed at the top of the door, and the waitresses in retro uniforms greeted us explosively.

"Hi! Welcome! Are you going to be joining that lovely party in the back corner?"

I looked back at the table with Frank's parents, and the glimmer in their eyes that seemed to have shown through the window was now painted over with a more muted glean, with hushed exchanges and subtle nods.

"Yeah, that's us!"

Frank bound toward his parents, arms outstretched. I lingered a few steps behind him, ready to time my arrival perfectly to walk into a shy introduction.

Frank motioned that his parents needn't stand up to greet us as I approached the table.

"Mom, dad, this is Catherine. She's the one I've been telling you about."

Frank's parents exchanged knowing looks, having heard about me from Frank prior, knowing that Frank had been in a relationship with somebody. Something told me that he had intentionally left out specific details, like my age, and perhaps other traits that would have given any indication to my personality or what I looked like.

"Oh!" his mother said, politely surprised. "Aren't you beautiful?"

She glanced back at Frank, who beamed proudly, looking toward me. Frank's father stared at me as well, and with three sets of eyes on me, mine fell to the floor. I blushed and shook my head, lifting my eyes to the table to say I was pleased to meet them.

It was my general go-to for people to assume I was quiet and reserved when I first met them. I never felt the need to come on too strong, or to put any foot forward. I thought that if I could come off as a muted version of myself, it'd be difficult for people to dislike me. The best part being that if, in the future, I decided to feel more comfortable with those around me, they'd then be shocked to see I was decidedly not the person they thought I was. I could always chalk it all up to me being nervous the first time I meet people.

Even though it was calculated. Even though it wasn't true.

Frank and I slid into the booth, me sandwiched between him and his father. I made eye contact with his mother, who looked away quickly, as though I had caught her doing something she shouldn't have been doing.

"So, Catherine. I heard Frank took you through his childhood home! What'd you think?"

Boring. "It was great."

I thought about the different ways in which it was actually good, and added, "I especially loved seeing all the pictures."

I knew this'd be a good opportunity to make an impression, showing that my favorite part of the house was them, and their memories. I stole a glance from Frank, who looked taken aback. His eyes brightened, and I knew I'd said the exact right thing.

"My favorite photo on the wall is the one of Frank and the rest of his siblings in Germany." his father considered.

"Oh! I think I remember that one." I lied

"Yeah, their grandparents—my parents—would take them to Germany every few years since they were kids."

At this point, Frank interjected to add, "Like I've said to you many times before, Catherine, I just feel like travel is very important. Everyone should do it. Everyone should seek these experiences."

Before I could stop myself, I heard words spill out of me.

"Well...that's not fair, is it?"

Frank and his father both stared at me, incredulously.

"What do you mean?"

"What do you mean, 'what do I mean?'" I pressed. "It's not like you decided that at an early age. Your grandparents and parents exposed you to that. It's not like you asked for them to take you on these trips. You didn't know that it was important until someone else provided that experience for you, repeatedly."

Frank's father gaped at me, and then turned his face quickly toward Frank, awaiting the rebuttal.

Frank began to scramble a bit, unaware of how to proceed. I felt as though his quips in class, his one liners, were never actually challenged, and this was unfamiliar to him, never having had to defend himself.

"Well, you know, I just feel that travel is important and… and that people should find a way to travel one way or another. It doesn't have to be the most expensive by any means, or the most luxurious travel experience."

"You're still not understanding how privileged that is to say, though. Not everyone knows that that's an option for them, especially those who may not have had a lot of money growing up. I know you're not saying that everyone has to splurge when they travel, and I know that traveling can be affordable. I also understand that there is so much culture to be learned about, so much of humanity to experience, but if you live paycheck to paycheck, that's something that's so out of reach for some people. Mix that in with the fact that maybe their parents didn't instill that value in them, and then they were never able to save enough to even have this in the back of their minds. I don't even think you realize how what you're saying is a little problematic."

Frank's father laughed jubilantly, completely entertained by our exchange. His eager eyes wanted more, and he looked between Frank and I expectantly, waiting for me to continue on my rant, or for Frank to try to defend his point.

Frank's frantic gaze softened as he heard his dad chuckle. It annoyed me for a second, the thought of him using his dad's lightheartedness to dissolve the conflict. That he wouldn't have to admit he was wrong, or even really learn from the experience. He would be able to cast it aside, and move on to looking at the menu, and showing me off to his parents. It bothered me that he didn't seem able to admit that he was classist in any particular way because he'd built his identity as a worldly, accepting individual.

"So, did you guys already order?" Frank inquired, not even the faintest rattle or quiver in his voice.

He was so unashamed in blatantly changing the subject, and I had to wonder if he'd even fully realized that I was right in what I was saying. Had he even listened? His parents said they hadn't and lifted the menu up slightly from the table to glance down at it.

"We'll probably just end up getting what we always get. What do you guys want?"

I brought the menu up to my face, my eyes burning as I scanned it. How many times had they been to this diner? How many different dishes did they try before they had a "usual"? How many different things does anyone need to try before they know that they don't need to try anything else, forever?

"Are you folks ready to order?"

My tablemates shouted out their orders in a rehearsed order, and finally all eyes were back on me.

"Do you have any daily specials?" I hoped.

"No miss, the menu hasn't changed since 1969! We value tradition here. Hope that's okay!"

"Of course that's okay!" I replied politely. "I was just checking my options here. I'm sorry, I've never been here before."

"Take your time, dear. We got time. Everyone here always knows what they want, it's just that kind of a place."

I gave the menu another run through, trying to find anything to catch my eye. A soup of the day. A pie that was the chef's choice for the week. Anything on a rotation that didn't feel like it was set in sealed plastic for all of eternity. My stomach lurched, and I started to feel nauseous.

"Actually", I said. "I'm sorry. I'm not really feeling up for food. I'll just stick with water for now."

Frank drove me to the airport the next day, and I joked about how I'd be seeing him in a few day's time. Being in California was Frank's final trip of the summer, and once he'd returned, he'd only have a few days before the school year started. I thought back on the summer that was finally coming to a close. The trips, the emails, the exchanges, the memories we'd experienced together, good and bad, all the same hidden versions of me, with all the different versions of Frank.

I turned to Frank, who'd been distracted by the traffic.

"What if I looked completely different by the time you came back?"

He scrunched his face up in confusion. "Different, how? In what way?"

I toyed around with the ways in which Frank looked different over the summer. Frank with long hair. Frank with short hair. Frank who'd lost weight. Frank who'd gained weight.

"Well, what if I just got really fat?" I joked.

Frank's eyes widened. "I feel like it's not in your personality to let yourself go like that."

Surprised by his unwillingness to play along with the hypothetical, I pressed.

"Yeah, but just, what IF I did? Would you say anything to me about it?"

I truly was just curious at first, but after his initial response, I did feel more inclined to pry.

Frank's face somehow found shadow in the sunroof-lit car, and tilted his head toward me without looking directly at me.

"You wouldn't do that." He muttered. "You wouldn't do that to me."

I furrowed my brow in disbelief, staring at him. I looked out the window, straight ahead, and fought back the urge to scream. I stole a side glance at his waist, his stomach spilling over his light wash jeans with a belt that was too dark to match, and whipped my head toward the passenger side window, tears of disgust and frustration flooding my eyes.

In the comfort of my apartment, alone, I had known for a while now that I'd be moving. I just didn't know when, and I didn't know where. I did now.

Confirm Payment. Payment Confirmed.

Bad News

Turning the card over in my hands, I eventually let it plop to the floor. I flipped my body over to stare at the ceiling, hoping the dramatics of my actions would incite some kind of reaction. Some kind of effort of trying. Some kind of triumph. Some kind of umph.

It felt good, to have a direction, to have made a decision, even though it didn't have to be for forever. I never had to be certain of this choice, vacuum and pressure sealed tight. My choice was a flavor of the week, month, or year. It was written on a dry erase board, announced to the staff, but could be erased and rewritten at the whim of the eccentric CEO. I licked my lips.

"Hey, CCC. Guess who's home?"

I read the message over on my phone, remembering I'd told him I'd be busy today and thus unable to pick him up from the airport. I couldn't remember what excuse I'd used to weasel my way out of giving him a ride home, an endeavor I'd offered eagerly every time prior. That excuse decidedly hadn't been that I'd needed to buy a ticket to move out of state, away from him, away from us.

"I guess that'd make the both of us? Hahah."

I replied, hoping his response would give me a hint as to what I told him I would have been doing.

"Oh! Finished up early? Well, come join me for a drink when you can!"

No luck. I looked at the time, noting that it really didn't matter what time it actually was because I'd always be willing to drink when presented the opportunity. I told him I'd be over soon, and without even giving my reflection a glance, I snatched my belongings and walked out the door.

I parked my car in my usual spot at the curb in front of his house, and peeked into his window. I noticed his curtains were pulled tight over the windows, no hint of a light shining from the other side. Even with no sign of life, I strode toward the door, checking the handle boldly before letting myself inside.

The light in the living room was off, however I could see the kitchen light simmering from behind the TV. I set my bag down on the couch and crept toward the kitchen to see if Frank was busying himself in there. Rounding the small corner, I noticed he'd had put some items out from his liquor cabinet, another little build your own drink bar prepared neatly on his kitchen countertop. Assured that Frank wasn't anywhere in the lower level of the house, I quickly grabbed the bottle of gin, spun the top off, and took a large gulp. I winced and tightened the cap, and decided to venture upstairs. Any regret or shame I felt washed away suddenly.

"Uh... hello?" I bellowed.

I heard creaking from the bedroom, so I began my climb, each step making my presence more and more pronounced. Halfway up, I called out again, hoping to hear some kind of response. When greeted once again with silence, I quickened my pace and found myself staring into his empty bedroom.

I saw his suitcase in the corner and his jacket tossed onto his bed, so I knew he'd made his way home from his trip. The quiet was shattered abruptly by a muffled grunt, and I jerked my head to the closed bathroom door to my left. Shit. He was in the bathroom. I didn't know how much of me he had heard from there, or if he knew I was in the house at all, but I knew waiting on his bed to surprise him would have been the worst move possible.

I imagine how horrified I'd be if the person I'd been longing to see all summer had been waiting patiently outside the bathroom door, like a loyal pup, greeting their loving owner after taking a massive shit. I decided to tiptoe my way back down the stairs. I grabbed my bag from the table, scrambling for my phone to text an alibi. Frank hadn't said anything about letting myself in, or that he'd otherwise be temporarily occupied.

"Hey, I let myself in. I'm gonna fix myself a drink!"

Feeling like my bases were covered, I stood up buoyantly and bound over to the kitchen. Scanning the bar, I couldn't decide what I'd wanted to drink, or even how to make fancy drinks. The well mixes that were usually on happy hour menus seemed easiest, but I was excited by the assortment of things in front of me, wondering what I should whip up for myself.

But first, another shot.

Then, a vodka martini.

I wanted something simple, strong, and also something to snack on, so a dirty martini felt like a good place to start.

Two ounces of Grey Goose. Two ounces of vermouth. A hefty splash of olive juice. Ice. Mix. Pour. Three olives. No, one more. And one for the walk back to the couch.

I sat on the couch, waiting for Frank. I checked my phone to see no reply, and resigned myself to waiting in the dimly lit room. Not wanting to busy myself too much with my phone, I set the glass on the ground and extended myself on the couch. I stared at the ceiling, wondering when best to tell Frank that I'd be leaving.

He'd had an idea that my internship had ended, that I hadn't really been searching for any work. I propped myself up on my left arm to grab my drink. I wasn't sure what he'd really expected of me, and we hadn't really had that discussion of what would happen once school would resume and I wouldn't be joining the others. It felt strange that the seasons, the semesters, would no longer mean anything to me.

I lifted the glass up to my lips, and briny, rubbery stoppers bounced off of my teeth, with no other liquid seeping through. Huh. My drink is empty. I reached my fingers into the glass to fish out the remaining olives and popped them into my mouth. I stared back up at the staircase, seeing no visible sign that Frank would be joining me any time soon. I stood up and bounced toward the kitchen, enabled by the freedom I'd had to the alcohol.

Two ounces of vodka. Two ounces of vermouth. A hefty splash of olive juice. Ice. Mix. Pour.

I looked at the jar of olives, which was nearly full when I'd arrived, and was alarmed by how it seemed to be edging on the halfway mark. Two olives.

I sat back down on the couch, and heard the unmistakable sound of a toilet flushing. I sighed in relief and awaited Frank's descent.

He seemed genuinely happy to see me, his eyes glittering in the dark room.

"You didn't want to turn on the lights? Or watch some TV or something?"

"No..." I lied. "I'm perfectly content as is. Welcome home!"

I stretched my arms out wide, his one person welcoming party. My drink sloshed in my hands, some of the concoction catching in my hand and dribbling down my arm.

Frank sat down next to me and gave me a soft, warm kiss. I pushed into him, unsure of how I was feeling or why I wanted to feel his face on mine.

"Whoa," he said, taken aback. "Like the ocean. And a pirate. Are you okay?"

"Yeah! I'm just getting started."

Frank looked at me suspiciously, and walked toward the kitchen. I saw him eye the olive jar a bit longer than I'd have liked, him trying to recall how empty the jar had been before I arrived. The jar had been opened, I remembered, because it didn't make the sound it does when seals break, so I felt confident that at least an olive or two had been eaten at some point in the past.

Frank began to move slower than usual, his movements seemed distracted, as though he needed to work something out in his head before rejoining me on the couch.

Finally, drink in hand, he sat down carefully next to me, and looked deep into my eyes.

"Catherine, Catherine... my parents were very impressed with you."

I had thought that he was going to comment on the fact that I was glaringly drunk, but then realized that, perhaps he was using this opportunity to open up to me in a way that he might not have felt comfortable had I been sober. Now that I no longer had the capacity to be the person who'd talked to him and treated him how I had in California.

"They're very nice." I slurred.

"They were really taken with how you and I were bantering, how you jabbed me. I think they thought, you know, because of the age difference, that I was somehow dominating you or taking advantage of you. They were really happy to see us together, and how we interact."

I nodded absentmindedly, and kept nodding, like a swing slowly winding down from the momentum even after someone leaves it. How frustrated had I been? How unseen and unheard did I feel at that table with his parents? People who didn't understand the point of what I was expressing, but just watched me perform for them, merely for their enjoyment.

Briny rubber bumpers knocked into my teeth again, and I let them plop into my mouth, chewing largely.

"And they were actually. Well, they wanted you to... I mean, they wanted me to invite you to come with us on this family trip we're taking to Canada in October. All of us are going. Both of my brothers and their wives, and my parents wanted me to extend that invitation to you. All expenses would be paid, of course, if you can make it."

I stood up, and wobbled over to the kitchen. A couple of glugs of vodka. A little splash of Vermouth. A lot of olive juice. Some olives. No ice. Swirl around. Pour. Sip so that the glass doesn't spill on my way back to the couch. Sit.

Frank stared from me to the glass and continued where he left off. Or maybe, he had jumped onto another topic. I wasn't sure.

"School starts next week, as you know, and so my schedule will be a bit hectic at first, but things are finally slowing down. We're finally going to be able to actually spend time together, to enjoy ourselves."

Sip. Olive.

"And with that, I mean, my schedule will settle down. We can settle down."

Sip.

"You know, I never thought it'd be possible for me to have kids. But now, with you, I realize it's still in the cards for me. I really never thought about it before, not recently at least, not since my divorce."

I stared down at myself, my lap, where I'd sloshed some of my drink onto me. Drunk and terrified of his words, I hated him. I downed what was left in the glass and fished out the olives with my fingers and strutted back over to the kitchen, chewing loudly on the way. I found myself once again, staring at the line of bottles. I placed the martini glass in the sink and grabbed a water glass. My crotch was still uncomfortably wet, but I knew that I couldn't do much about it at this point.

Grey Goose. Seagram's Extra Dry Gin. Peppermint Schnapps. Maraschino Cherry juice. No ice. No mix.

I stumbled back over to the couch, feeling prepared to resume the conversation. Frank's face contorted, his brow furrowed in a pleading way. I felt myself swaying on the seat next to him, and took another sip of my new drink. I happened to sit in the same spot I'd spilled my previous drink in, the couch cushion soaking through the back of my pants. I glared down at my lower half.

My head was spinning. Is that what he saw? That I was just some young, fertile uterus that could give him something he'd initially thought was no longer an option? I crossed my legs uncomfortably, thinking that that was all of me that he saw. The only part of me that he wanted.

This entire time, I thought I'd been using him, that he'd been helping me sneak my way into a life I hadn't yet earned. A life I longed for, but never wanted to work for. And yet, it didn't occur to me that he could have been doing the same to me. Striving for a life he thought he had been too late for, a train he couldn't hop onto in time.

I took another gulp of my drink and set it down, my head swirling. I set my head down against the armrest.

"Catherine... What are you drinking?" I watched him reach across the table and lift the drink to his face.

Frank winced. "This is fucking disgusting."

"I don't want kids." I said.

"Let's get you upstairs."

Frank let me hang on to him as he led me upstairs and into his bed. I collapsed onto the bed, the room spinning around me.

"Wait." I slurred, "Bathroom."

I made my way to the upstairs bathroom, and crawling to the toilet, I just made it in time for my face to projectile into the bowl. The taste of alcohol, peppermint, and the searing sugary cherries was offensive on all parts of my tongue, and I retched louder into the toilet, echoing around my face. I forced myself up from the amphitheater, and flushed the toilet, my arms guiding me toward the sink. I'd had my own toothbrush, so I rinsed out my mouth and watched my reflection as I brushed my vomit-coated teeth.

The mirror showed me, my ruddy face, my blood-shot eyes. Behind me, the door. Behind that door, I'd know what was waiting for me. That room, that man, that conversation, that future. None of that was what I wanted. And yet, there was the door beyond that, the one that led to the stairs. The stairs that led to the door outside.

Outside that led to ambiguity. I knew that I'd have to go into the next room in order to get to where I really wanted to go. There was no way around it. I finished brushing my teeth and, still drunk and spinning, laid back down on the bed.

Frank was beside himself with grief.

"Catherine, are you okay? I'm trying to have a serious conversation with you, and how did you even get so drunk? Why did you even get so drunk? I'm telling you I want to finally start our life together, start a family."

"I said downstairs. I don't want kids."

Frank looked stunned. "You don't want kids." It was more of a statement than a question, but I still nodded.

"And I'm leaving."

Frank bolted upright.

"You can't leave now! Look at you, you're way too drunk to drive."

"No, I mean. I'm leaving. I'm going."

My eyes fluttering closed, I'd made no attempt to move, which assured Frank he didn't need to physically restrain me.

"Okay..." he responded calmly, knowing he'd have to be patient with me, well-versed with the drunken riddles. "Where are you going? And when?"

"I'm going, going, gone." I could feel the drool slip out from the corner of my mouth.

My eyes committed to closing, and for a moment, I heard nothing, saw nothing. I could still feel the wetness in my jeans. It wouldn't go away. And then, seconds later, the dampness began to spread, flowing out from me and spreading over Frank's bed.

Can't Stay

I was still not quite sure what was happening around me, but the commotion, the rapid movement, the panic Frank raised made me aware that there was a matter to be addressed, and even in my stupor, I knew I'd been the cause. I'd finally regained my ability to see the space around me, and I looked around at Frank, who had been making large strides around his bed, pulling the sheets and mattress covers from every edge and corner, bundling up the linens so that they wouldn't touch anything, only nestled in itself.

My head still spinning slightly, my brain still dim with my inebriation, I teetered downward to look at my body. I was sitting with my legs extended in front of me but I was leaning back while propping myself up with my arms, as though I were tanning by a pool.

Stranger than that, though, was that I was no longer wearing any of my clothing that I had been wearing as I laid down. I squinted at the bundle in Frank's hand, and noticed the leg of my pants sticking out of the crumpled sheets.

Then it hit me. I'd pissed myself in Frank's bed.

Frank seemed not to want to waste energy talking to me, racing against time to get all of his bedding into the wash as soon as humanly possible. I stayed perfectly still, wondering if I should play dumb or offer help. I decided to pretend to still be blacked out, waiting for Frank to clean up after me.

Frank rushed his urgent laundry downstairs, and threw everything in the wash before coming back up to help me rinse off in the shower. He hoisted me up with both arms through my armpits, and my feet began to find their footing underneath me. I found a hair tie around my wrist and threw my hair up into a bun, before stumbling into the shower.

Frank, seeing I'd regained some of my motor skills back, watched me cautiously at first, a child who had just gotten their training wheels taken off. I wobbled at first, but caught myself on the wall, and waved him off to signify that I could take the rest from here. He gave me a reluctant glance, and closed the door behind him.

Even knowing I'd pissed myself, I'd still had very little intention of thoroughly cleaning myself. I debated how much time would be enough to give the impression that I'd cleaned myself, but also didn't want to take too long to the point where Frank would need to check on me. I'd mainly wanted to use the time to let the water sober me up, as opposed to washing the remnants of my bladder off of my legs.

It occurred to me that I hadn't even been all that embarrassed by what had happened. Was it because it wasn't in public? Was it because it was only in front of Frank? But more importantly, was it because it was in front of Frank, and I didn't care what he thought about me? I tried to sift through the muddied memories of the evening, thinking about how drunk I'd gotten almost immediately after arriving at his house.

Why had I done that? Had he not been in the bathroom when I walked in, would all of this have transpired? I wanted to convince myself that it wouldn't have, that my actions and lack of self-control could be blamed on a singular incident that was outside of myself, but even as I tried to stuff that fake piece of logic into my puzzle, I couldn't make it fit. I thought about what I had done previously, about my past few days with Frank.

I had met his parents, had seen through the guise of his kumbaya persona he loves to tout. Had that been what put me over the edge? I hadn't put too much thought into who I thought he was before, but certainly getting to know someone at a deeper level opened up so many opportunities to find fault in them. Too many opportunities. Is that why I had gotten so drunk? I wanted to present more flaws to Frank? I had known all of Frank's flaws, everything I'd hated about him, but I hadn't considered what he could possibly have disliked about me. Was this a way for me to look detestable to him, to have him see me as I saw him?

My head went under the shower stream, which jolted me out of my thoughts. I slumped up against the wall.

"I guess that defeats the purpose of me tying my hair up."

I shut off the water and grabbed a towel.

"Okay," I whispered to myself, "Let's focus on what you can do now, going forward."

My head was already pounding, so the idea of sleep was first on the agenda. I wouldn't have to say anything to Frank until the morning. Next. What was next? I thought back to lunch... Frank's parents... and then I remembered the ticket. I had already mentioned it to him moments ago, as I was passing out, but he didn't know what I meant. He had little inkling as to what I was rambling about. I'd have to find a way in the morning to tell him I was leaving.

I walked back out into the bedroom as Frank had finished remaking the bed.

"Feel better?"

He seemed a lot more understanding than I'd have been in his position.

I nodded, and apologized. I popped back into the bathroom to place the towel back on the rack, and immediately crawled naked into bed. I looked up at Frank.

"Do you trust me to get back in here?"

Frank gave me a soft smile in reply, and crawled in next to me.

I woke up the next morning feeling as though I had been hit by a freight train. I was confused as to how I could have expelled fluids from my body uncontrollably the night before, but still feel like all of the consequences of my actions were bottled up within me. I turned to see Frank sleeping soundly, and standing up to use the bathroom, I saw a glass of water and a bottle of Tylenol next to me with a note.

"Catherine, Catherine. For now. For last night's mistakes. – me"

I smirked at the thoughtfulness, and unscrewed the bottle, popped two pills into my mouth, and gulped the water down greedily. After using the bathroom, I crawled back into bed with Frank, who woke up with a degree of urgency I'd only ever seen the night before in his efforts to change the bedding.

"Catherine, what happened last night?"

His tone sounded a bit frantic, and it made me uncomfortable to see him in a manner where he wasn't talking to me calmly. The patience he bestowed upon me the previous night seemed reserved only for someone unable to understand the damage they'd caused.

"I... I'm sorry. I got really drunk, and I just lost control."

This didn't seem to be enough of a reason for Frank, who continued to press.

"You know, I try to invite you on a trip with my parents. You just met them, and they really do like you! And then I start talking about our future together. You didn't even say anything to me, you just got up and made yourself another drink."

"Can we... I mean, I'm completely naked. Can we not have this discussion while I'm like this? I feel quite exposed." I felt it a reasonable request.

Frank stood up and went downstairs to retrieve my garments from the dryer. I tried to recount the events in proper order from the night before, and although I didn't pay enough respect to each of his prompts and questions, I knew that I hadn't said nothing. When Frank returned, I quickly dressed, some of the details slowly trickling back to me.

"That's not true," I challenged. "I said I didn't want kids."

Frank stared at me in disbelief, as though he had expected to paint the walls of my empty head with false memories of the night before.

"Well, okay, so you remember that. So, you meant that?"

I continued my eye contact with Frank. "Yes, I do mean that."

"I just, I thought we could finally start our life together, but it's really not a rush. I just realized there were so many things we can do together, that you make possible for me. We don't have to do it just yet, but in a few years, maybe..."

I couldn't let him dream any longer. I couldn't keep up the ruse. Even for me, this was exhausting, and I needed an out. I noticed on this side of the bed, I was closest to the door. Closest to the staircase. Closest to the exit.

I cut him off. "Do you remember the other thing I said last night?"

Frank's eyes burned into me as they held back tears.

"As you were falling asleep? That you were going? I thought you were just fading in and out of consciousness. What are you saying? What do you mean?"

When I was seven, I always enjoyed spending entire weekends at my friends' houses, spending the night, never wanting to be at home. My friends always had cooler things than I did, always had snacks, always had parents that seemed present and willing.

On one particular Sunday, my friend Hannah had her tennis lesson, so her mother asked me if I'd like to watch the lesson and then be taken home afterward, or be taken home prior to the lesson. Hannah's mother let me deliberate my options and left Hannah and I alone in the room while Hannah got ready.

"I think I'm going to go home before your lesson," I told Hannah, honestly.

Hannah began to cry, and I felt completely taken aback by her abrupt emotional reaction to me not wanting to sit on the bleachers for an hour and watch her play tennis.

"Never mind, I'm sorry. I'll go," I spat out, trying to resolve the situation.

Hannah stopped crying instantly and began to happily get ready again.

I had been so confused by the sudden change of her emotions, and couldn't wrap my head around why she'd wanted me there so badly, and also how she was able to alter her feelings at the drop of a hat.

"Actually, I'm not going," I tested.

And like clockwork, Hannah started sobbing again, her head in her hands.

"Okay, I'll go."

Hannah stopped crying and looked up at me expectantly. I smiled at her, and she smiled back.

"I changed my mind. I'm not going."

As Hannah burst into tears again, her mother walked back into the bedroom to see Hannah distraught and me sitting on her bed, my face looking withdrawn, detached.

"What's going on in here?!" she demanded.

"I… Well, I told Hannah that I didn't want to go to watch her play tennis, and that I wanted to go home, and she got upset," I stated. "And then she started to cry."

Hannah's mom looked at her daughter, concerned, but I kept going.

"So, I told her I'd go, so that she wouldn't be sad anymore."

Hannah's mother became more confused, wondering why her daughter had been so upset if she had eventually gotten her way.

But I kept going.

"And I didn't know why she stopped crying. So, I said I wasn't going to go, and then she started crying again."

Why had I kept going?

"So, then I said I was going to go, and so she stopped crying…"

Horrified and enraged, Hannah's mother stood up from consoling her daughter and approached me.

"So then, you kept seeing that one comment made her upset, and then kept saying it over and over again?"

My eyes widened. "I just wanted to leave, but I didn't know why she was so sad. I didn't want her to be sad. I said what stopped her from being sad, but I also wanted to leave, so I just kept saying what I wanted, but I wanted her not to be sad, and…"

Hannah's mother cut me off.

"You're leaving. Now."

I stared directly at Frank, and took a deep breath.

"I'm leaving. I'm not staying here, I just bought my ticket. I'm moving."

Frank's mouth opened, and I flinched, waiting for some kind of retaliation, the tears, the sobbing. The reaction that would make me lie to subdue him. He closed his mouth and began to breathe deeply through his nose.

"When?"

I went numb, knowing that all I had to do was get through this, the hard part, and it'd all be over. I closed my eyes for a second, thinking about the door behind me. It was so close. It was almost over.

Jump

"But that's in two weeks."

His response to my decision to move, although filled with whatever he happened to be feeling, be it anguish or despair, inspired nothing but anger within me. I dissected his words, diced them into indistinguishable pieces until I could use the detritus to kindle my flame.

Considering two key facts to the equation—the current date and the date I'd informed him mere seconds ago that I'd booked for my flight—it was needless to mention that I was, as it were, leaving in exactly two weeks. Though rage built steadily inside me, I knew deep down what he was trying to communicate.

We don't have much time left together.

Is there nothing else he can do to get me to stay?

He loves me and he's devastated that I'm actually leaving.

Truly, nothing he said would have mattered, though. Nothing would have changed my mind.

His words lingered in the stillness of the morning air, his gentle plea and my silence, tangled, suspended in the thickness of the room. I swallowed audibly, despite my parched tongue, to punctuate the awkwardness, as though any sort of utterance would buy me more time.

Lying in bed, facing each other, it occurred to me that we'd never quite seen each other like this before. Usually, I was on the other side of the bed, further away from the door, and as a consequence, I felt as though I weren't just looking at a different version of Frank, but staring at a complete stranger. My eyes scanned his body, from the crackling of his forehead, somehow exhibiting both signs of oil and dryness, working defiantly against each other, instead of one balancing the other out.

My eyes drifted to meet his, but just for a moment, as I was more intrigued by following the sporadic stream of tears gathered into the shallow oasis forming in the crook of his nose. Watching the trickle of tears pool slightly, I'd try to see if I could predict when the pool would finally overflow and slowly drip off the edge. Sometimes, though, the tears would somehow defy gravity and flow downward, finding their way sadly toward the cliff of his nose, only to hesitate slightly before committing suicide.

The desultory stream was enchanting. It made perfect sense at first, but as the minutes passed, my eyes began to process the tears as moving sideways, instead of downward. My brain pulsated in an attempt to normalize the anomaly, wanting so badly to accept something that didn't seem possible.

I was eight the first time I went through a car wash. I was with a childhood friend and her parents, and I remember how excited my friend had been to take part. Prior to this experience, I'd considered washing a car one of the most tedious chores anyone could be subjected to, but I feigned excitement to appease my friend.

"It's like being in a spaceship, ready to go to the moon!"

I smiled. At this, I, too, gained interest and found myself overcome with anticipation.

From the jump, it felt like we were ready for lift off. Lining the car carefully onto the tracks, being given the OK finger gesture by the carwash employee, and the light jerking that signified we were no longer in control of the vehicle. My friend's father even removed his hands from the steering wheel and made an animatedly shocked face, and looked back at us, as if to say, "look, no hands!"

We watched in awe as the swirling hues overtook the car, lathering and spreading, frothing and foaming. My favorite part, though, was after being completely doused in water, air suddenly blasted from all angles, creating the sound of an aircraft and simulating what I imagine is warp speed. I peered at the window and watched as the majority of the water vanished from the window in a shotgun blast. What clung to the window were the lowly remains. Or maybe, more accurately, the survivors.

The remaining beads of water clung desperately to the window, slowly being whipped away into nothingness. I'd been most enamored by these beads of water. I'd choose a drop of water to focus on, usually starting from the further end of the window—that meant it had more of a fighting chance to remain safe—and root for the little guy to cling to life as long as possible. Then, it was off to the races.

After watching for some time, my initial tactic was to choose the smallest water drops to place bets on, because the less volume it had, the less likely it was to be quickly flung from the window. In a sense, it could hide behind the weight of another, or due to its sheer insignificance. I'd surmised that, the more space a drop takes up, the more likely it is to get forced off the window's surface.

After observing these tiny particles of nothingness, I'd realized that my hypothesis had been correct. They didn't move, but they were decidedly less interesting to watch, so I'd drifted to the other contenders. The larger drops of water were more likely to be moved by the air, but they also seemed more likely to make it further in the race. The larger the drop, the more of a fighting chance it has at clinging to life. Maybe not in its entirety, but in the end, shedding the dead weight.

I'd thought that, as the wind attempted to whip the drop off the window, it'd leave a small trickle of water, but eventually reach the opposite end of the window, leaving a graceful snail trail gingerly treading behind. What I witnessed, though, was entirely different from the gentle movements I'd anticipated. I watched the rapid, staccato movements of the largest water drops spring up, down, at an unpredictable rate, buckling under the strength of the turbine. Sometimes, the droplet would even split, creating two new water droplets. At this, I wouldn't know which of the water droplets to root for.

My go-to would generally be the larger of the two droplets, but on occasion, I'd root for the little guy. Resorting back to my original tactic. Often times, though, the smaller droplets would just stop. They didn't have enough volume for the wind to pay any mind to them, or perhaps maybe for them to pay any mind to the wind. And at that, I'd thought, which is technically stronger? Although impressed by the smaller droplets' ability to sneak under the wind's nose, it occurred to be that there was truly nothing to watch.

Was the point of my game to see which water droplets would travel the furthest, or remain unscathed? Since it was a game I'd made up, I could determine its goal. Did I want the purpose to be to make it to the other side, or to remain stagnant? Was it truly more impressive to watch something so small, so insignificant, that not even the wind would want to blow it away? Or to be big enough to put yourself out there, to jolt, zig, and zag, break apart, fumble, fuck up, and yet, somehow persevere? Why was I so intrigued with this idea of remaining idle? Did I somehow trick myself into thinking that hiding and being sneaky, deceitful, and untrustworthy was something to be admired? Why was I so against being so brash, and bold? That it was somehow clumsy, and ungraceful, and.

"Unbeautiful…"

I watched his mouth part away from the recent string of suicides, slightly to call out for me, let in some air, quiver, and let out a soft whimper. Lying on his side, I watched his jowls slump towards his pillow as his tongue lobbed around his mouth. As he finally closed his muzzle, I scanned his clothing, which were always comically unstylish.

I shut my eyes animatedly, like a child hearing a strange and unexpected noise, praying the monster to go away. I wanted so badly to disappear. As quickly as I'd shut them, my eyes bolted open. I raised my manicured finger to tuck my hair behind my ear, and felt the suppleness of my skin. I slowly brought my knees up toward my chest, and forced my eyes to meet his once again. The tears subsided as he began to see my mind had wandered, as it does. It had been wandering. As he knows it does.

He'd been alone, crying in bed, as I penetrated his sadness, diving into the depths of his despair, a voyeur in his ache. Not to understand, not to comfort him, but just to observe.

As much as I was very much in the room, and as much as I'd wanted not to be, he'd wanted me there with him in bed, and yet, I wasn't. It was in this instance that I realized I was incapable of giving either of us what we wanted. For myself, because it was impossible, and for him, because I was unwilling.

"Yes, that would seem to be the case." I finally managed to uselessly sputter out. I paused. "But I'll be here for your birthday."

I knew this reassured him little, but it was the kindest, most truthful thing I could say to him. At this point, my words could only do so much to mask my actions, and it felt more disrespectful to continue lying any further.

Frank spastically lifted his massive hand up, which caused me to tense. Visibly, I think. Slowly, then, he slid his baseball glove over my face, caressing me, where I had just moved the hair behind my ear. He stared deep into my eyes, searching, as I fought the urge to smack his weathered mitts away. His hands weren't painful by any means—or perhaps, not in the literal sense—but they were unpleasant, and I cringed with every one of his longing strokes.

The touch of his hand on my face reminded me of a cheap, worn towel. Not completely useless, but grainy, threadbare, and unable to live up to its full potential. Kept around for the sake of not wanting to throw something out. Who knows? Maybe you'll still get a few good uses out of it. When something's purpose is utility, it does make it difficult to get rid of unless you've sucked it dry. Is its useful life really and truly over, or are you somehow afraid to part with it?

I could feel him wearing down on my skin with each stroke, unraveling. I was raw with his efforts, feeling him crumble as he tried to look for me. I sank further into myself as he dove in to find me, losing more of himself in the process.

And yet, he persisted.

"Rin..."

It took me a minute to recenter my gaze to meet his, his words like a microscope, auto-adjusting itself under my eyes, moving closer and further away from him, attempting to find the perfect focus. My eyes adjusted to his pixelated outline, dilating in and out, while I finally brought my eyes to meet his.

His blue eyes were soft, loving. They were yearning for me, loving me, and I could barely stand to look at them. I could have spent more time swimming in them, admiring and appreciating them, as he did me. Instead, I wanted to follow the stream of tears, and jump off the cliff, and leave him for good.

Was I truly stagnant, though? Was I hiding behind my own insignificance? Or had I started off larger, bolder, strong, but now smaller, having shed the nonessentials along the way?

He'd turned his hand to graze my face, the corner of his jagged thumb nail catching on my cheek. I flinched, and met his eyes.

"I love you," he'd said.

He always said it first.

Everyone always says it first.

Why did everyone always say it first?

"I love you, too."

I almost always said it back.

I'm almost always lying.

Why do I ever say it back?

His eyes seemed to soften as a flow of deep understanding washed over him.

"I've been gone a lot this summer," he'd considered. "And when we started this thing, of course, neither of us had planned it. My schedule was full, what with the conference, and the trips..." He trailed off, started again.

"I know now. You've been chasing me all summer, and now it's my turn to chase you."

I let out a little laugh. I thought he'd understood what I was doing, but really, he was searching for reasons to fit his own narrative. I smirked without thinking, and he seemed pleased by what he considered a smile.

My eyes fell from his mouth, my gaze flowing toward the bottom of the bed, and I slowly untucked my feet from the fetal position. My outstretched legs longed for the edge of the bed, working their way down, left, right, treading, squirming and inching until I could feel the corner of the mattress. My toes gripped the edge, and relief washed over me. I glanced once more into the shallow pools that dripped with sorrow, took a deep breath, and looked back down over the edge. An eerie breeze washed over my body.

Then, I jumped.

CPSIA information can be obtained
at www.ICGtesting.com
Printed in the USA
LVHW030158070423
743755LV00005B/233